READER PRAISE FOR
GEORGE BYRON WRIGHT'S NOVELS

Baker City 1948

"I just read *Baker City 1948*. I was absolutely knocked out! It is one of the best-told tales and interesting books that I have read in years."

— Jim Helliwell, Roseburg, Oregon

"Beautifully written with great attention given to plotting and pace. *Baker City 1948* had me absorbed to the very end. Philip's voice and perspective had the appropriate combination of simplicity and emotion. By the end of the book, I felt I had a solid grasp of the entire Wade family, not to mention the town of Baker City in 1948."

— Hunter Gregg, Portland, Oregon

Tillamook 1952

"[Wright] dealt well with the mystery of the plot and the setting while developing a character who is able to grow and change with his experiences. I liked that; a man's story that is able to explore the ability or inability for people to relate to each other. Thanks for a good story!"

— Janice Nichols McLemore,
Silverdale, Washington

"[Wright] has human emotions entwining and erupting like flames sliding up the trees of the Tillamook Burn... Anger and guilt and love rise like the heat of the fire and are just as difficult to control... Wright's skillful use of narrative takes the unrelenting curiosity of a man who has been shielded from a dark secret and carries it like a burning torch to a terrible conclusion."

—Bob Olds, Reviewer, *Colonygram,*
Oregon Writers Colony, Portland, Oregon

Roseburg 1959

"What a skillful and engrossing read. I thought the resurrection of Roseburg and Ross Bagby were a necessary commentary on small-town society and the state of marriage today. I too was surprised at the end ...it was a masterful touch to the intrigue of characters."

—Max Penner, Kansas City, Missouri

"*[Roseburg 1959]* was a great story, with interesting, likeable (and some unlikable) characters, good villains, a few surprises, a satisfying ending, a sense of 'place,' and a hint of a love story. I enjoyed every minute I spent reading it."

—Teresa Edwards, Vancouver, Washington

Driving to Vernonia

A NOVEL

To Mary Ann

Driving
to
Vernonia

A NOVEL

all the best!

[signature]

GEORGE BYRON WRIGHT

11-5-09

C3 Publications
Portland, Oregon
www.c3publications.com

Driving to Vernonia, a novel.
Copyright © 2009 by George Byron Wright.

C3 Publications
3495 NW Thurman Street
Portland, OR 97210-1283
www.c3publications.com

First Edition

Library of Congress Control Number: 2009905984
ISBN10: 0-9632655-5-5
ISBN13: 978-0-9632655-5-5

Cataloging References: Driving to Vernonia
1. Men and jobs–Fiction 2.Divorce–Fiction 3. Mentors–Fiction
4. Elder Abuse–Fiction 4. Oregon–Fiction I. Title

Book and cover designs by Dennis Stovall, Red Sunsets, Inc.

Cover photo by Dennis Stovall, Copyright 2009.
Author photo by Sergio Ortiz: www.sergiophotography.net

Driving to Vernonia is a work of fiction. Names, characters, places, and incidents are the product of the author's imagination or are used fictitiously. Any resemblance to actual persons, living or dead, events, or locales, is entirely coincidental.

Printed in the United States of America.

Books by George Byron Wright

Fiction

The Oregon Trio
Baker City 1948
Tillamook 1952
Roseburg 1959

Driving to Vernonia

Non-fiction

The Not-For-Profit CEO: A Survivor's Manual

Beyond Nominating: A Guide to Gaining and
Sustaining Successful Not-For-Profit Boards

"An obligation to persons lost to you is the saddest of debts to have. You cannot change the weight of what you owe them. You cannot even thank them. You cannot ask for their forgiveness. You cannot say goodbye—unless they be found."

—Anonymous

To
"Dick Van"

Acknowledgements

While writing a novel is very much a solo process, eventually I have to invite people into my little world to react to what I've come up with. The initial step is asking a few trusted souls to be my readers; they are presented with the raw words, full of flaws and often far from what the final work will be. So thanks to my wife Betsy, who always gets to see the original manuscript. Thanks for her patience and loving encouragement. Thanks also to Michael Hosokawa and Greg Nokes for being early readers and gingerly giving some needed reaction to that first draft.

Once again I owe a debt of thanks to the Portland State University (PSU) Publishing Program and the spring 2009 book editing class, led by instructor Vinnie Kinsella, for critiquing this novel. Their input led to many changes and improvements in *Driving to Vernonia*. Special thanks go to Karen Brattain, my extraordinary editor, for deftly guiding me to further hone, refine, and correct the manuscript.

Thanks to Dennis Stovall, Director of Ooligan Press and Co-ordinator of the Publishing Program at PSU, for lending his formidable talents to the design and formatting of this novel.

George Byron Wright
Portland, Oregon
August 2009

Mentor Lost, Mentor Found
THE MOTIVATION FOR A NOVEL

Driving to Vernonia became the germ of an idea when I rediscovered a man of great importance in my life after a twenty-five-year lapse. I first met Richard VanOsdol in 1955, when I was fifteen and we were both working for Bergs Supermarkets in Salem, Oregon. Dick Van, as he was nicknamed, was produce manager for the store where we both worked: I boxed groceries at the check stand, stocked shelves, and, among other duties, packaged eggs.

When sorting eggs, my companion in that back room was a tall, gangly young man who sorted and processed fruit and vegetables. He was ten years older than I was, had attended Willamette University in Salem, and would regale me with his insights on philosophy, the Civil War, and other heady topics. There, among eggs and eggplant, we had great discussions and became great friends.

Then I graduated from high school, attended college in Eugene, Oregon, and Dick and I lost touch. However, when I married and returned to Salem looking for work, Dick, who had since become store manager of one of the Bergs stores, hired me on as a grocery clerk, and we were reunited for the first time.

It was during the next three years of working for Dick that he became a mentor and role model to me. Being a mentor is not something anyone plans: mostly the person isn't even aware of his or her role in someone else's life. And I'm sure it was like that for Dick Van back in those early days of the '60s. Dick's impact on my life was absorbed day by day: no lightning bolts, but moments of strength, empathy, guidance, humor, and above all— generosity of spirit and a giving of self.

I left the grocery business for good in 1965 and saw Dick only once more before losing track of him for over twenty-five years. I never thanked him for his impact on my life—an omission that haunted me for years. I would try to find him every once in a while, but without success. I didn't know where he was. Finally, I devoted the time and energy to really do the job and found Dick Van back in Salem, right down the road from Portland, where I lived. Our reunion was a high point for both of us—and I finally got to thank him personally. We soon began having monthly lunches, and afterward, we would sit in his car and have long discussions about life: its challenges, its highs and lows. Most of all we deepened our friendship.

Shortly after finding Richard again, I was intrigued by the odyssey of searching for someone misplaced but not forgotten. And, soon, I began drafting a novel in which finding someone long lost is vital to salvaging a life gone awry. Thus emerged Edmund Kirby and eventually *Driving to Vernonia*—all thanks to Richard "Dick Van" VanOsdol. I must caution that this novel is not about Richard VanOsdol; it is a work of fiction, but it was inspired by my lifelong friendship with him—though many years lapsed.

Are there people in your life whom you have misplaced and perhaps never got around to thanking for whatever it was they did to make your life better? I encourage you to find them. If your mentor has since passed on, thank his or her spouse or offspring.

So once more: Thank you, Dick!

George Byron Wright
August 2009

<driv•ing to Ver•non•ia> *v phrase:* the act of locating a person of significance in one's past.

-1-

My downward spiral began with the divorce. That's going on seven months ago. If I go all the way back, I suppose I could blame it on my sky blue 1950 Nash Ambassador Airflyte—at least partially. That homely hunk of steel, dubbed the *upside-down bathtub* in its day, had a split-back front bench seat, and both halves could be reclined into a full-sized double bed—truly a modern miracle. And when Sylvia and I tested out this ingenious feature, which was often, I gave a silent prayer of thanks to those visionary engineers at Nash.

Even on that particular night, Sylvia and I had again enjoyed the comfort of the Nash at a favorite spot off old Germantown Road on the outskirts of Portland. But it wasn't until we were in her parent's driveway that my life objectives slid away like a rude guest. The old car's stilled engine was ticking in the warm night air when Sylvia gripped my arm, fingernails digging in, and announced with emphasis: "Edmund, I'm pregnant." Everything I'd planned on, much of it somewhat underway: those anticipated carefree days of young adulthood, my college years, a degree in business—for which I had great hopes—that all evaporated in one wide-eyed moment, a moment engraved on my brain like a bad debt. It was the middle of August 1972.

1

Sylvia was staring at me, the porch light casting a pasty whiteness on her face. "Edmund," she said, her brown eyes waiting, "what are we going to do?"

Indeed, I thought.

Hence came my big life lefty, as I called it. Goodbye to college; all eighteen months I had in by then, after waiting two years to get started—that was over. We debated how to keep me in college and start a family; but we had no luck, no rich parents, no scholarships, nothing. So zippo to college, then a quick I do, sign on as the breadwinner, hunker *down* and take on life. That's what you did back then. I'm not saying we were unique in experiencing this age-old dilemma, just that it happened to *us*, damn it all. At twenty-two, I was caught trying to go up the down escalator. Sylvia at nineteen and still flush with her own idyllic dreams, must have had regrets the moment we were legit and she saw me yawning and scratching in the morning. Sure seems that way in retrospect.

———————

From a quick weekend honeymoon on the Oregon coast in the Nash until our recent ugly patch of road, Sylvia and I, we racked up twenty-seven years. At my age, a man is supposed to be cruising right along: building up his retirement, at the peak of his earning years, an empty nester—or close to it—and mostly at peace with life. I'm not cruising anymore. It's over and can't be fixed. I've replayed everything that happened, gone over it and over it. It's broken and must have been mangled for longer than I knew. I'm talking about the marriage, but there's more to it.

Like I said, after living with me for more than half my life, she walked away—Sylvia. Every other person I know tells me I must have seen it coming. No. Maybe I was numb to it. I mean, we did the right thing: got married to save everyone embarrassment from the outcome of those enjoyable trips in my Nash, and then settled in. Seven months later we had the child; we named her Samantha. Had it been a boy, I was all set to name him Nash— Sylvia said not on my life. By the time Tommy came along eight years later, I'd forgotten the Nash. Turns out that Sylvia and I played the role: we went about life—job, kids, household—and I guess I was the one who shuffled along in a groove while Sylvia was doing a fair amount of pretending and not getting what she wanted. I assumed that she loved me, that we were the real deal, family, support, respect. Hell, I guess even our pretty good sex wasn't…pretty good. Anyway, I had a life. Now I don't, but I'm dealing with it, in my own fashion.

Take today, for instance. It's ten o'clock right now, Wednesday morning, if I'm right; and I'm still in bed. A world-weary thirteen-inch RCA television is perched on a chair close enough to where I can reach out and flip the channels—no remote. Martha Stewart, her face an orangey green, is doing something clever with an empty tomato juice can. And Elvis save me, I'm thinking of what I might do with the two soup cans I tossed last night. That does it.

I flip off the television, sink back against two lifeless foam pillows, and watch a spider scooting across the bumpy ceiling. The whole apartment has cottage-cheese ceilings with glittery speckles embedded in it—an obvious touch of class. When I say *whole* apartment, I'm really referring to this cigar box of a bedroom, a bathroom where your knees meet the wall when you're seated, and a combination kitchen and living area. My sister calls it a collage of inconvenience.

I'm going back over my situation again, thinking about synergism—you know, simultaneous action, the greater effect of separate elements when they are combined? Always been a believer in things acting differently if they're thrown in with other things. Now I'm damn sure of it.

———

There I was, Edmund Joyce Kirby-Smith, with a wife, two grown kids, house, two cars, riding lawnmower, drift boat, and a good job with Singleton Wholesale Foods. At least that's the way it was last summer, the summer of '99, when everything was still in place, neat and comfortable. I was closing in on my fiftieth birthday, married for twenty-seven years, and I'd been with Singleton for over twenty. Numbers like that, they can send you a message, but I didn't pick up on any implications. It's spring now, the spring of 2000—the new millennium. It has been a little over six months since Sylvia pulled the plug, and I still swing from being filled with rage to silently mourning.

It was last September when Sylvia left and never came back. Every year she would go off to visit her sister for week in Seattle, forever and always right around Labor Day. This time she didn't come back home to Portland, the bowling ball that never returned.

Anyway, on that Sunday, the day before Labor Day, Sylvia called, caught me watching the Seattle Seahawks being thumped by the Dolphins in Miami. She asked what I was doing. I said, "Watching football."

"Oh. Well, I'm staying for a few more days," she said.

"Why?" I asked innocently.

"I just feel like it."

"Well, okay, I guess. When you coming home?"

"I'll call," she said.

I yawned. I do remember yawning—was that calm about it—said okay, and that was that. We hung up like it had been a telemarketing call for cracked windshields; neither of us said *I love you, goodbye* or *how are you doing?* That's the way it is between marrieds sometimes—I'm not condoning it. It just gets like that, comfortable—okay, complacent. Of course I regret it now, I mean not saying something more to her, because come the Thursday after Labor Day I got a registered letter from some

4

attorney I had never heard of. Sylvia was filing for divorce. In a panic, I tried to call her; but her sister, Sandra, or Sandra's husband, Bill, always answered and in slow, sad voices said Sylvia didn't want to talk. Their voices became less sad and more clipped after fifteen such calls.

Finally she relented and talked to me.

"Sylvia?"

"Yes."

"It's me," I said, trying to keep from screaming, *What the hell!*

"I know, Edmund."

"So, what's going on?"

She sighed—a long sigh, I remember. "You got the letter? From Jeffrey Blaine?"

"I got it," I said. "Damn right I got it. Big fat envelope from… what is their names again?"

"Blaine, Hoskins, and Davenport."

"Yeah them. Syl, why…why are you doing this? What do you mean *irreconcilable differences?* What's that mean?"

"It means I don't want to live with you anymore," she said quiet-like.

"Just like that."

"No, Edmund. Not just like that." Her voice rose then. "Not just like that. This has been…well it's been coming for a long time."

"I see." But I didn't see. "How long have you been planning this?"

"Edmund, please let's not…"

"Let's not what, Sylvia? Let's not act like this is a big deal? Let's not act like this hurts? Let's not act like my wife of twenty-seven years just walking away is not a frigging big deal? Let's not act—"

"Edmund! Stop."

So I did—stop. My heart was pounding. We didn't say anything for a long minute or so. We didn't hang up on each other; we just waited. Then I could hear her crying.

"Syl," I said quietly, "are you crying?"

"Of course I'm crying," she said. "This is awful."

"Then why do it?" I asked.

"I have to." That's what she said back to me. "I just have to."

"But why?"

"To save myself," she answered. "Goodbye, Edmund."

That's the last time I've spoken to her in all these months, the very last time. Right after that I spent days and nights reliving our lives, what our lives had been like, at least in my memory, and looking for the bad spots. They were there, all right, but I had paved over them. Sylvia and I had hit the wall more than I realized. The hardest times had always been over our kids. Raising children isn't easy, and we had our share of small wars over kid issues. A few days after we'd talked, the cold chill of old recollections came to me. Times, so clear now, when Sylvia gave me clear warnings, but they were warnings I never absorbed. Once, after a tough round over a clash about Samantha, Sylvia stood with her back to me and said: "I don't know how long we can go on". I guess the signals and the self-fulfilling prophecies had been there, I either ignored them or just put them away.

As bad as the divorce was, I would have been all right, well, at least tolerable, if that had been all there was to my downward spiral. Once I had gotten myself upright after talking with Sylvia, I called the kids right away. But it was too late. Sylvia had forewarned them; in fact, they knew before I had even heard from her lawyer. Samantha, the oldest, lives here in town. She's married to a very successful hard-ass venture capital guru, no kids, and—as it turned out—no real sympathy for her father.

"You weren't really surprised, were you, Dad?" my daughter asked me.

"Yes, Sam, I was surprised."

"Really? Well, I have to go along with Mom on this, sorry. It's the right thing."

"What do you mean by that?" I asked.

"You and Mom had what I'd call an empty-calories marriage, Dad. Shouldn't have to live a whole life on empty calories," she said.

"What's that mean?" I remember squinting while I waited for her answer.

My daughter laughed. "Yeah, I guess you wouldn't be the one to grasp that, now would you? Tell you what, Dad, it'll be over soon. Do what Mom's going to do, reinvent yourself and enjoy life."

We haven't talked since, Samantha and I. Then again, we have more baggage than a few teenage skirmishes with her father and the divorce of her parents. My biggest claim to fame with Samantha is my adamant disapproval of the man she married. I didn't much like the young man who showed up in our home carrying an ego the size of a small planet, a man who looked down his nose at my position as distribution manager of a small grocery wholesale company. He had bigger plans. I took it personally, I'll admit, but I didn't trust Phil from the moment I met him. I didn't like the way he lorded it over Samantha, and I made the mistake of telling her so. She cried for three days over that blunder and later on barely let me give her away at the wedding. I guess the divorce gave her the rare opportunity of rubbing her father's nose in his own failure.

It wasn't a whole lot different with Tommy, except he seemed a little sorry. I suspect his smidgen of pain was more fear that maybe there wouldn't be money to keep him in Corvallis at Oregon State University in the style to which he'd become accustomed. I caught him in the dorm on a Friday just when he was heading out for the evening. I could hear it in his voice that his mind was elsewhere.

7

"So you knew about this, Tommy?" I asked.

Behind his hesitation I heard hyper male voices, young testosterone ready to bay at the moon. "Yeah, I did," he answered. "Mom called me awhile back. Told me she was gonna do it."

"Shock, huh?" I said hoping to nullify Samantha's body blow.

Another pause. "Not really, Dad. Mom hasn't been happy for a long time, I guess. Look, I have to go."

I can still hear the drone of the dial tone disconnects from those two calls.

The divorce, it hollowed me out, but it was really just the first peel of the onion. I had always thought of myself as made of strong stuff. I can even remember pitying those I judged to have given up when hit with a setback; I smirked at their waffling and whimpering and caving in. I never imagined having days on end when I didn't want to get out of bed. But that's where I've been.

Anyway, I managed to layer on some crocodile skin and adjusted to living in this apartment hive with strangers coming and going and shared laundry and shared garbage and shared parking, though I have no car—I made that adjustment, barely. I'm living out here in north Portland because this pile of boxes has space I can almost afford. And because, you see, not long after the divorce, the next peeling came—onion-wise. Singleton Wholesale Foods had been family owned for over seventy-five years. Werner Singleton, grandson of the founder, was running the company; but none of his offspring cared enough to get their hands soiled in a tough, competitive, uncool business. It was barely two months after my divorce when old man Singleton announced his retirement and sold out to Amalgamated something from Ohio. The company held a shindig in celebration of the new ownership, wining and dining all the employees, thirty-five of us: pickers, loaders, salesmen, managers, drivers, and secretaries. We ate bloodrare steaks, drank earthy red wine, and spooned up succulent chocolate mousse. Grinning, joking fools—that's what we were, backslapping over the good times ahead. A big company had bought us out—greater opportunity lay just ahead.

The following Monday, Werner Singleton took his distribution manager—yours truly—out to lunch at his country club and told me Amalgamated would be bringing in its own management team. I was out. Wasn't even offered a sales job.

The onion was peeled.

-2-

According to the divorce decree, Sylvia and I were to split the equity on the house. We'd lived there eighteen years, so we came out okay. Sellers' market, good location, we did very okay. Sylvia left Portland and moved to Seattle, taking most of what we owned to furnish her new life—supposedly one with more calories to it. I rented a small U-Haul truck to move what was left, and here I am.

The final peel of my onion is that I'm without a job, living on the remaining months of unemployment checks and a modest ten grand in savings (my half of our nest egg). Time is running out. These days, I look at myself in the mirror and don't recognize the puffy-faced person staring back. It is frightening how little time it takes to lose one's spirit and, worse, to then adopt it as okay. Do I give a damn? Not today. Time for coffee.

I'm tossing a coffee filter filled with second-run grounds in it when the doorbell starts dinging its starving gerbil squeal. I open up, half expecting someone sent to save my soul. We stare at one another like strangers for a long moment before I walk back to my make-believe kitchen and spoon fresh grounds into Mr. Coffee. She comes in, clunks the door closed, and comes right up behind me.

"Aren't you all gussied up," she says, obviously put off by my fashion statement: no shirt, sweatpants cinched below my belly, pillow hair, and bare feet.

Sugar is my sister, my only sibling—my little sis. Regina is her given name, Regina Anne, a name never used. Our father doted on her and her sweetness and called her *Sugar* from the start and forevermore. She stands five foot four to my six feet, has a sweet pink face, a blonde head of hair that is cut short, and is forty-four to my forty-nine. She's married to Robert Carson, nicknamed *Salty,* and so go the unending jokes of *sugar* and *salt.*

"Coffee?" I say. "Ready in a minute."

Sugar sighs and drops her purse and coat on the couch, one of four pieces of den furniture donated to me by the court. "A cave," she says in a flat, brittle challenge. "Criminy, it's like living in solitary confinement. Light, Edmund, light." She yanks on a curtain cord and blasts open the drapes; dust flies. The confines are shocked into brightness. I see no improvement except I have to squint now. Sugar purrs. "That's better. Light, you need light for life, Edmund."

"If you say so."

"My god, look at you." She holds out her arms and hands like scythes. "It's nearly noon. Don't you ever get dressed? And cleaned up?"

"I am dressed." The coffee maker is gurgling behind me.

"And you're getting fatter."

She strides up and slaps me on the belly. Stings. She stands with her feet apart, hands in fists on her hips. Sugar's set on fixing me, has been ever since she heard that Sylvia had had enough of me.

"You should have seen it coming, Edmund," she'd said back then. "Mile off you should've seen it. Sylvia has been hankering for something more for years. And you aren't something more. You're solid and faithful but not something more. Not the right

11

woman for you. Never was. Time to shed your skin and start over with someone else."

She was in my face the day after I was laid off at Singleton's, too. Same thing. "No biggie," she said. "You can do better than that place. Always thought so. You weren't right for that job—a paycheck was all it was."

Isn't that the point? Thing with Sugar is that her wanting the best for me ends up being that I'm not fit for anything I've been doing for the last quarter of a century. Her free tutorials were always insightful, and they always stung. It's not that she doesn't care for me; she loves me. I know that, but her analysis is always tough. So I'm a dull guy who married a woman I could never have satisfied with the libido of Rudolph Valentino and slaved at the wrong job for decades and probably shouldn't have expected otherwise in either case.

"Don't know how you can stand this place." Sugar turns around in a complete circle. "Stifling. No room to breathe."

"I don't need more room, and I can breathe fine. Coffee's ready. You want some?"

She waves me off. "No. Edmund, what are you doing? Where's your drive? Your pride?"

I pour my cup full and turn to her and muster up the trace of a smile. "Still sorting things out." I take a sip of coffee and study the astonishment on my little sister's face.

"You've been sorting for nearly six months. How much sorting do you need?" She re-examines where I live, turning, looking. "You need plants in here, something alive, something green."

"I'm alive," I say, "and there's something green in the fridge." My humor is wasted.

"We're going out for lunch." I just look at her and swallow more coffee. "I'm paying," she says, "if that's what that look is. Now get dressed."

I can't refuse my little sis, never could. As I stuff myself into some lifeless khakis and blue polo shirt, I can hear Sugar trying to rearrange my living quarters. I chuckle, slip on a pair of tired loafers, and think of being Sugar's big brother. I used to be her protector, the one to intervene with our father when she wanted to wear lipstick, the one she ran to sobbing when she didn't make rally squad—that's who I used to be. Fact is, she went out and married me. Old Salty reminds me of me when I thought I knew who I was, but he was smart enough to marry a woman who wanted him just as he was. I figure I'm scaring the hell out of Sugar; she has to be wondering if Salty would fade away like I have if hit with a big setback.

She pops up off the couch when I come out and looks me over. "That's okay, I guess. You ever iron anything?"

"What, we going to a four-star restaurant? Got my blue blazer, could put that on."

"I'm just wondering if Denny's will let us in." She heaves a big one and yanks the door open. "Okay let's do it, brother of mine."

We're halfway across the courtyard of the apartment complex when I see the wide body of Felix sitting on one of the benches that are scattered sparingly around the grounds. He's leaning forward, elbows on his knees, feet hidden in the spring grass, smoking a cigarillo. You could say that Felix Saguaro and I are confederates. He's my only social contact these days. I met him at the garbage bin shortly after moving in, and we found each other's demeanors to be without stress or unwarranted expectation. Saguaro isn't really his last name; it used to be Williams. Says he ruined that one and always liked the sound of Saguaro and the solitary nature of those huge cacti. A fine fit he said. Felix and I, we aren't friends in the real sense; we're just mutual practitioners of disengagement.

As we pass, Felix taps the ash off the end of his cigarillo, looks up at me, and raises his eyebrows. I smile and shrug as Sugar marches by with me in her wake. He nods and looks back down at his feet. I don't have to give him some smarmy greeting and introduce my sister then make insipid comments about the weather or nice to meet you and all that.

Maybe I'll fill Felix in later about Sugar and my trip off the grounds. Neither of us goes off site much, so he may be curious. Then again, maybe not. That's how it goes with Felix.

The waitress we draw at Denny's holds a pen over her order pad like a court reporter and stares hard at Sugar, who is vacillating over which delicacy she wants from the plastic-coated menu. The young woman inhales and sulks. I want to tell her it doesn't matter, take it easy, no one really cares if my sister takes another twenty seconds to choose between a chef's salad and a taco salad. Then she decides on the mandarin chicken salad anyway. The smile from the waitress is more like a grimace when she says, "Good choice."

"So, Edmund, time to get it together." Sugar is short to begin with, but she also has a runty torso and appears to be sitting in a hole, her chin only inches above the tabletop. Makes no matter; she is too tough to let her shortness hold her back.

"Wouldn't you say?" She leans into her words.

"So for the price of lunch at Denny's, I get to be a punching bag?"

Her fingernails are talons on the table; she does the finger drill, her red nails clicking like castanets. "What is it with you?" she says. "Why are you quitting like this? Criminy, a lot of people run into a bit of bad luck. Most scratch their way out of it and get on with life. You know? Start over, get mad, get glad. Make a move here, Edmund."

"Shug," I say with a sigh, "look, I'm doing okay. I'll be okay."

Sugar sits up and licks her lips. For, I don't know, maybe half a minute she doesn't say anything. Her expression of puzzlement is a flashback; I can remember that look on the face of the little girl I once knew.

"You're scaring me," she says. "You know that? You're being totally strange."

"What's new? You always called me weird."

"We were kids. This is different. I need to know if you're okay. You've been really through it. I know that the divorce, losing your job, that'd put me down. Put anybody down. For a while. For a while it would, but...seeing you just quit, living like you are...I'm afraid."

The waitress suddenly appears and deftly forearms our orders onto the table. Sugar inspects her chicken salad then compares it to my bowl of chowder with side of cornbread and a small iceberg lettuce salad with ranch dressing.

"You left out near bankruptcy and my alienated children," I say and blow on a spoonful of lumpy soup. "Not to mention a total destruction of a social life, loss of friends and the like. Left all that out."

"So, that's it, then? Why you're acting like a bloated sausage?" Sugar picks over her salad, finds the chunks of chicken, and shakes her head. "Poor me, that it? Criminy."

"I'm learning things," I say. "For instance, just today on television I learned something you can do with a tomato juice can. What you do is—"

"Stop!" She slams an open palm down, the plates and utensils jump, and heads swivel in our direction. She leans forward and whispers hoarsely. "How can you let yourself go to pot like this? You're driving me crazy. People are asking if you're all right. It's embarrassing."

"So this is about you?" I break off a chunk of cornbread and dab some butter on it. When I look up her face is red and her eyes are wet. "You know, you can just let me do whatever, Little Sister, I'll wash up on a beach somewhere. Don't you figure?"

Sugar sets her fork down and squeezes the paper napkin into a ball. "Edmund," her voice is so small, "I can't…I love you…my big brother…I can't just wait and see if you can get upright again. What if you don't?" She dabs her eyes with the napkin ball.

I shrug and lower my spoon into the chowder again. "I've never not had to perform: as a husband, as an employee, a father, socially, good neighbor, friendly fellow about town, dutiful—all of it. There's a kind of serenity when there are no expectations of you."

Sugar is looking at me, her fork suspended with a chunk of chicken clinging to its tines, her eyes wide. "Can you hear yourself?" she says.

"What do you want from me?"

I watch as her face flattens and loses its bloom. She sets her fork down. "I want you back," she says. "That's all, Edmund. Just come back."

I spread more butter on a hunk of cornbread and don't respond.

"Is it Sylvia? Is that what this is about?" she asks.

"You mean the woman who wasn't right for me, Shug? That one?"

She smiles a little. "Guess I was too blunt on that one, huh?"

"History," I say. "Besides, it's over…over and done."

Sugar gives me a tight, skeptical smile—one that is so familiar—and takes a drink of ice water. We concentrate on our food for several beats.

"Really?" she asks. "No leftover stuff."

"I guess I hated her at first," I say, breaking the quiet. "For messing things up."

Sugar keeps her mouth shut.

"Then I wake up alone in my bed and…that's when I know she's really gone," I say. "At first when that happened I actually felt a surge of panic."

"About her being gone?"

"About being alone." I laugh. "Silly, a grown man."

"Still, it must be really strange," she says, "I mean, after all those years."

"First night in that apartment? That's when it dawned on me. Really hit me. Until that day, I'd never lived alone. Never been just by myself. I'd either lived with you and our parents or with Sylvia and the kids." I take in a shaky sigh. "Whew."

"What?" Sugar leans toward me.

"Haven't said that out loud before."

Sugar sits up as straight as she can and drops a hand on the tabletop. "Well, we'll just have to—"

"No," I say. "No fixing Edmund plan. No."

"Edmund, you need to—"

"I don't *need* to anything."

She sags back and looks even smaller. The waitress strides up and begins clearing the table. She asks if we want dessert; we say no but both order coffee. We sit without speaking until the coffee shows up. I drink mine black; Sugar adds cream and artificial sweetener.

"Maybe you need to talk with someone," she says, stirring her coffee until it turns the color of caramel.

"You mean like a shrink?"

She hesitates, looks out the window. "No, I can't see you doing that," she says turning back to look at me. "Would you?" she asks hopefully.

"No."

"Who would you talk to, then?"

I raise my cup and sip coffee. "Talk to about what?"

"I don't know," she says. "Maybe you need someone to just listen."

"What, to me whine?"

Sugar sighs and studies my face; there's a wrinkle between her eyebrows. "Haven't you ever told someone how you're feeling?

17

You know, when you're down, have a problem. Have you, Edmund? Ever?"

I cringe. "Like who would I bore with my sob story?"

"A friend," she says, like I ought to know.

I can only lift one shoulder and shake my head. "No friends," I say, "at least none I'm going to let inside my head."

We sit quietly and take occasional drinks of our coffee. The waitress cruises by and drops the bill next to me. Sugar reaches over and takes it, gathers her purse and extracts a credit card, all the while studying me.

"What about that guy you used to work for?" she says. "You know, a long time ago?"

I chuckle. "Could you be a tad more specific? Like what lifetime?"

"Oh, you know the one, when you all worked at that Bob place?"

"Bob place? What…oh, you mean Bob-Buys?"

"Yes, that's it," Sugar says. "What was his name, the man you worked for there?"

"Richard Vickerman," I say. "Dick Vic, as we called him."

"Yeah. You used to talk about him all the time. Dick Vic this, Dick Vic that. Whatever became of him?"

"I don't know," I say. "Lost track of him."

"What about him, Edmund?"

"Him what?"

Sugar inhales, exasperated. "Someone to talk to about…about your situation."

"What's the point?" I ask. "To hold hands and sing 'Kumbaya'?"

"Criminy, Edmund. He's someone who meant something to you, isn't he?"

"Shug, give it a rest," I say. "I'm not wired like you."

She pays for lunch like she promised, my sis.

-3-

The oversized radiator fan of Sugar's Land Rover roars and thrashes the air. She white-knuckles the wheel, fights back more tears and anger and deposits me back at the apartment. I stand in the heat from her exhaust, hands in my pockets, watching the white, upscale suburban transport vehicle until it exits the parking lot, listing slightly. I doubt the machine has ever truly been off road. All that potential will remain just that—potential. I laugh; that SUV and me have a lot in common. Criminy.

Felix isn't hunched over on the bench anymore, but he never goes far. I spot him across the yard on the northwest corner of the compound's x-shaped sidewalk. His profile is that of a much older man; his back is slightly hunched, coupled with a shuffling walk. A forward lean gives the false impression that he is a person in a hurry. I raise a hand; he spots me and keeps his unhurried pace. I stand by the bench with my shoulders rolled forward and shudder as the spring sun begins to warm the top of my head and shoulders.

Felix ambles up; we flick our eyes at one another and sit. He leans back; I lean forward. In our silence the sounds around us rise up: a truck gearing up off somewhere, a door slamming, the damn crows sitting up in the fir trees cawing at one another.

A lawn mower coughs then revs up and begins its drone, smoothing out into a rhythmic hem and haw. The Hispanic fellow has his own little mowing business; he comes by as often as the landlord will let him and mows the apartment weed patch like it's worth it. I saw his mustard-colored International pickup with the splayed wooden sideboards when Sugar let me off. The sound of the mower begins wearing on Felix. He re-crosses his legs and folds and refolds his arms a couple of times. The mower is closing in on us.

"It won't be long now," I say.

He grunts, again.

"Want to go over to my place?" I offer.

Felix looks over his shoulder toward the advancing mower and grunts.

"I have some beer."

Felix sniffs. "Got beer," he says and waits a beat, "and a balcony."

I've been able to get Felix into my place only a couple of times. Of course, I have a lousy television; plus, I'm on the ground floor. He's on the second floor with a balcony that looks out over the common area for this quadrangle of four-plexes. Felix likes to sit out on his four-by-six balcony, stare down into the scruffy green space, and watch the comings and goings and fussing of the other inhabitants. The drone of the mower is louder, chewing its way toward us.

Before it closes in, Felix shoves off. I follow him up to his apartment; he pulls a six-pack from the fridge, and we settle into aluminum deck chairs on the balcony. He hands me a no-name beer, the cans hiss open, and we suck off that first foamy swallow in unison then settle back and watch the yard guy who is just now mowing around our bench.

"We cut out just in time," I say.

He nods, drinks some more and goes silent. It's odd being with someone on a more-or-less regular basis who you sort of know but don't, not really. I guess Felix to be about sixty, sixty-two maybe. He's obese and shaves maybe once a week; his hair's gone on top and hangs in lanky strands on the sides. I have no idea what he used to do, if he has family, how he supports himself. He's never asked me anything personal, either.

"Sister?" he says right then, making me out a liar.

"That's right."

"Figured. Resembles you."

"Not a chance," I refute.

He shifts in the chair and says, "Round the chin and the nose. Eyes a little, too."

The mowing guy stops, levers the machine into idle, unhooks the catcher, and walks off to empty it into the bed of his truck. The pungent smell of sliced grass rises up. There's a certain peacefulness that comes from watching someone else work at something you could be doing but aren't. I think of all the acres of yards I've mowed in my lifetime: mowing, edging, fertilizing, watering—mostly so I would be seen as a good neighbor.

When the yardman comes back, I take another swallow and say, "I don't see the likeness."

Felix wipes the sweat from the can on his pants leg. "That's the way it is with family. Don't see their own selves in each other."

The mower revs up again, bogs down, and drones on.

"She's not happy," he says.

"We have our moments, especially these days."

Felix is chatting me up—imagine that—way out of character. I'm waiting him out; the yard fellow finishes up, and the place is calm. We each open another beer.

"Not high on your exotic lifestyle, I'll bet," Felix says at last, "your sis."

"She is worried," I say. "If her big brother can hit a downer then who knows? Maybe her man's next."

At this moment, a young woman emerges from her ground-level apartment across the way. She's an instant distraction: tall, blonde dye job, makeup you can see from a hundred yards, skin-tight white pants and a red sleeveless top that's stretched out nicely. This female, we call her Lolita, she stops like always and checks for an audience, spots the two oafs on the balcony, repositions a purse strap, and sets off on tall wedge shoes. We both tilt forward to catch the rearward action of her ball-bearing gait before she goes out of sight.

"If they find out about her, they'll raise our rent," I say.

"Tenant retention," says Felix.

We sit like immigrants from Easter Island watching the afternoon drift by until the tenants with real lives reappear, returning from offices, machine shops, beauty parlors. They're carrying sacks of groceries and plastic bags of dry cleaning; they're limping, plodding, fatigued from another day out there.

Finally the complex is quiet; all the bees are in their hives. I stand and rub my behind with both hands, trying to get some feeling back. "Come on over to my place. I'll cook up something." I don't know what, though.

"Cook?" Felix's stomach bounces with restrained mirth. "Like it here," he says.

"What about if I order in, then," I offer. He's agreeable.

Duke's Pizza delivers within thirty-eight minutes. We dine on an extra large pepperoni and cheese and share the view of our cliff dwelling. There is nothing but crumbs left when we shove up from the chairs and go inside. Day is done, show is over. In the calm of Felix's apartment, which is a clone of mine in reverse, we sit swallowing back cheesy pizza memories.

"Thanks," he says after a bit. "Not half bad."

"My pleasure," I respond. Cuisine is our strong suit.

Felix reaches out and pinches a table lamp on then thumbs the television remote (baseball, Mariners and the Angels), mutes the sound, settles back, gloms his eyes on to the screen.

"Scares her then? Your sister," Felix says.

I'm looking at him, bewildered. He has never asked me anything personal. It is an oxymoron, that's what it is: putting Felix and nosy in the same frame.

He clears his throat loudly and sniffs. "Been through it," he says without looking my way.

"You've been through what?" I ask.

He chuckles. "Upsettin' folks, family mostly."

"Why? Because of the way you're doing life here?"

"Yeah, that's got it, *doing life*." He chuckles, eyes still on the ballgame.

"Did they get over it then? Your family?"

"Yeah," he says. "Mostly. Looka that." He jabs a finger at the television. "Godamighty pull the guy he can't pitch a dime's worth."

So much for Felix's self-revelation. We sit like usual, taciturn, closed-mouthed comrades sharing nothing but air. The game is in the sixth now, Mariners up by three runs. A Viagra commercial comes on. Irrelevant.

"May I ask what happened? What changed for...in your life?"

He blinks. "You can ask," he says.

"But you aren't telling?"

He clamps his front teeth onto his lower lip and bites down until there are teeth marks when he lets up.

"Lost my mojo," he responds finally.

"What's that mean? You lost your job, that it?" I say.

He sucks air back through his teeth. "Yep, lost my go-to place. Told me I wasn't welcome no more, couldn't get up every day and go do what I did for all those years."

"What was that?" I ask.

Felix just stares at the television.

"Never mind," I say, "I just thought..."

"Metal fabricator," says Felix. "Eighteen years. Eighteen fucking years. Could do it all: weld, form, bend, drill, cut...all of it."

23

"What happened?"

Felix leans his head back and closes his eyes. "Cost 'em fifty thousand. That's what they said: lost fifty thousand. One job."

It's quiet. The television flickers with fastballs and foul balls. Felix opens his eyes and gapes at the soundless ballgame.

"First screw up in eighteen years." He rubs his hands over his face. "Drill settings were off three-hundredths of an inch. Might as well have been a mile."

He looks at me. "I was down the well in hell. Down the well, and there was no me anymore, anymore. Stayed down there, too," he laughs. "Took early retirement, and here I am."

Game's over; Mariners win. Felix punches the remote right into the silent mumbling of Peter Falk in a *Columbo* rerun.

"And feeling fine as frog's hair," Felix says, nodding, agreeing with himself.

Laughing voices rise up from outside through the open sliding door to the balcony. I'm glad somebody's enjoying themselves. Felix scoots off the couch and takes a trip to the john. I watch Peter Falk wander about in his old trench coat until Felix is back carrying a fresh beer. He scoots his butt around on the couch, pops the tab on the beer can, and settles in.

"My sister thinks I should talk to someone," I say.

"Uh-huh. Like who? Shrink?"

"No," I answer. "A man I knew years ago, a man I worked for."

"And who's this fella to you?" Felix's eyes are focused on *Columbo*.

"He was a good man. Guess you'd call him a mentor."

Felix laughs loudly. "A mentor! Gonna hold hands and set things right?"

I feel a flash of anger and the need to defend Richard Vickerman, a man I haven't seen in two decades. Instead, I lean back and keep my mouth closed while Felix finishes his beer.

"I did that once," he says, breaking the quiet. "Looked up a guy I knew just after getting the axe." He chuckles. "A mentor."

"So how did that go?" I ask.

Felix lays his head on the back of the couch and looks up. "Stoddard," he says. "That was his name. My metal shop teacher in high school. Was him that gave me the idea of working in metal. He encouraged me. He egged me on, made me take on tough projects and told me when I did good. The only person who ever did that." Felix paused. "Anyhow, after they kicked my ass off the job, I looked him up. Tried to, anyway. Didn't know if he was alive or not, he was pretty old. But I found him, down in Salem."

"Not far, then," I say.

Felix barks out a hard laugh. "In the correctional institution."

"In prison?"

"Damn right. Fucker was in there for molesting kids."

"You go see him?"

"Yeah, I did. Saw the old fart. He cried like a baby when he saw me."

"So he remembered you?"

"Oh yeah." Felix snorted. "Asked for me to forgive him. Said he'd be out in six months and hoped we could visit. I told the bastard I wasn't gonna do any such a thing.

"So there's a mentor for you," he says. "The bastard made my decision for me, and here I stay. Anyhow, that's how it's done. Now, this is over. Go do whatever." He hits the remote, and the sound comes on. *Columbo* credits are rolling; *Murder, She Wrote* is coming up.

-4-

It's a quarter to eleven, day two after my séance with Felix, and I'm slicing a banana for my favorite food group: peanut butter and banana on white bread. Between conflicting scenes of Sugar and Felix, the positive and the negative, I shave thin banana slices and consider Sugar's idea about looking up Richard Vickerman. I can actually conjure up an image of Richard's face, locked in a time warp, a man of maybe forty-seven or forty-eight, like he was last time I saw him. I count on my fingers and calculate that it has been twenty-five years at least since I last saw him.

He was slender, wore short-sleeved white dress shirts that were always a size too big, topped off with the company-required red, clip-on bow tie. I'm smiling at the picture in my head of his long face, big teeth, prominent Adam's apple, and that wide mouth with pale thin lips, so pale they seemed to disappear, and that on-the-sly smile. Back then he had black, wispy-thin hair combed straight back, glistening with Brylcreem, and a thin mustache trimmed so very precise: straight and exact.

This memory is like mental paint-by-the-numbers. Richard's eyes were narrow crevices with blue peeking out, like he was sneaking up on you. He could slice and dice with those eyes, though, chop you up or prop you up. The nose. Just a nose, slender, no lumps or bumps, with a delicate end and subtle nostrils.

He usually wore a gray tweed jacket; put that jacket on him, and viola!

Damn, there he is. I can see him just as he was—Richard Avery Vickerman, or Dick Vic to anyone who knew him at all. Now what? Go find him? Then what? Tell him of a grown man's failings? He would always listen to me when I was sixteen; that all seems so inane now. But back then everything was monumental to a teenage male: girls, sex, my parent's rules for me, more sex and girls and all the other horrendous setbacks that seemed so devastating—traumas of the moment. None of which I could discuss with my own father, who wasn't a bad man, it was just that for Richard everything was so clear.

My first high school job was at Gilson's Superette as a bagger and stocker. Dick Vic was the assistant manager and had the thankless task of not only managing the store's daily operations but also calming the sour, hard-nosed Mr. Gilson, a man with no sense of humor who treated his employees as disposable and untrustworthy. It was Dick Vic who ran interference between the old man and the rest of us who worked there. When Mr. Gilson would confront me—*What are you doing there?*—which he did often, and not just to me, it would be Dick Vic who would step in and calm the moment and guide Mr. Gilson off on another matter.

Mr. Gilson left the store every day promptly at three o'clock. From then until closing, Gilson's Superette was alive and fun, with Dick Vic joking, laughing, and helping bag groceries. I guess that was when I came to revere the man and to begin asking him things—about my life. Many nights after closing, when he and I would be the only ones left in the store, we would sit on case goods in the storeroom and just talk. He'd loosen his red bow tie and light up a cigarette. Sometimes he joked and laughed about Mr. Gilson; other times he would listen to my hesitant questions about my parents, a crisis with a girlfriend, or other such momentous issues. So yeah, I'd say I idolized him.

27

The phone's ringing. I lick peanut butter off my fingers and yank the yellow Princess phone off the wall and grunt into the mouthpiece. It's Tommy. Always a glad-sad thing when any family calls these days. Guess it's still nice to be remembered, but with Tommy there's always a hook.

"Hey, Tommy," I say, raising my voice, wondering—knowing he wants something.

"How's it going, Dad?"

"I'm getting along, son. How about you?"

"Good. School's good, you know."

"Glad to hear it." His voice sounds huskier, more assured. Reminds me that I haven't seen him in person since the day he left for Corvallis.

He coughs into the mouthpiece; I recognize this sign of nervousness. "Hey, Dad." Here it comes. He never calls just to touch base; the fact is he never calls. "I was wondering…what I mean is I hate it in the dorm."

"That so?"

"It sucks. It's noisy. Hard to study and get any sleep." I'm thinking I can give him some lessons on sleeping. "Anyway," he goes on, "I have this chance to bunk in with some guys I know… in an apartment."

"Well, if you can work it out." I'm playing with the boy, forcing him to spit it out.

"Well, um yeah but, Dad?"

"Uh-huh."

"The guys share the rent and everything."

"Sounds right."

Tommy grows silent on the phone, and I can almost see him rolling his eyes and shrugging to his buddies like, *How thick can a guy be?* "If I do it, Dad, I'll need some extra, you know, for my part of the rent and all."

"Yeah." I'm grinning.

"I was wondering if you could help me with my share of the rent."

I don't say anything, imagining my son looking at the wall, his head pressed hard against the earpiece. "As I recall, Tommy, I paid everything up front for the full year. We sold the house and took most of what I got out of that for your tuition and all for the year."

"Yeah, but."

"Including dorm expenses. So you have a roof over your head all paid up."

I hear him inhale; he is exasperated. "Dad, this is a great deal—my share will only be about two hundred a month. Dirt cheap."

"It's up to you, of course," I say, innocent as hell, "but I can't pay twice for your rooming down there. I suppose you could get a job and pay for it that way. Guess I'd just lose what I've already advanced for the dorm."

"Dad, I can't flip burgers and keep my grades up. Won't work."

"You may not like the idea of a job, but you'd better think on that. Next year you'll need some student loans, maybe apply for a grant or two, and hold a job to get through. There's not going to be money for a full ride next year unless your mother can do it. I just won't be able to."

I can hear him breathing, holding back until he can't. "Yeah? Well…what about if you get off your butt?"

"What did you say?"

"Look, I know what's going on," he says, his voice lowered like someone might be listening. "It's embarrassing. The whole family feels that way."

"Is that right?" I say.

"Flat doing nothing," he says. "Come on, Dad, get some pride."

I feel a flash of heat but manage to swallow it. "Uh-huh. Well, I've been through a tough stretch here, what with the divorce and my job being sold out from under me. I think you know that. So I'm sorting things out. Now it's your turn to sort out where you're going. I suspect if you're smart enough to make it in college, you can figure out how to make it the rest of the way. Lots of your fellow students are working their way through, I guarantee you."

"Hey, Dad…uh, look, I'm sorry," Tommy says, backtracking. "But I really need some help. You're planning on going back to work, aren't you? Then things will be like before, right?"

"Nope, they won't be."

My son is speechless. "Well, fuck," he whimpers, "what am I gonna do?"

"You're sitting on a mountain of knowledge—it's all around you. Go find out what to do." He breathes; I breathe. I say good-bye and good luck. Tommy is still pleading as I hang the Princess back on the wall.

I'm standing at the kitchen counter eating my sandwich, washing it down with a cold glass of milk and considering my son's estimation of his father. I can only hope that he finds a role model to look up to, maybe a college professor who sees all the potential Tommy has, the potential I saw but never got around to encouraging. It's ironic that I'm thinking about relocating my own role model, thinking of really searching for Richard Vickerman.

I make another peanut butter and banana sandwich then go get my stamp album out of the bedroom closet, bring it back to the kitchen table, and lay it down gently. It was really my grandfather's stamp collection; he left it to me in his will. I'm no stamp collector, but I enjoy just leafing through the pages, looking at the colors and the history. The album is the one family artifact that gives me comfort and transports me away from my cheerless days.

Right now, I'm opening Grandpa Kirby's stamp album to occupy my time and my hands while I think, thumbing the pages, gazing at bits of color from long ago: *1947, Thomas A. Edison, heliotrope, great American inventor, 3¢.*

I could try and locate Richard; I could try.

Casey Jones and Railroad Engineers, 1950, brown, 3¢.

"Hello, Dick Vic, remember me?" I say out loud practicing.

I'm finished with my sandwich and my muddle. I wipe my hands, gently close the stamp album, and return it to the closet. I toss the banana peel and take my overly ripe garbage to the Dumpster. I'm waiting behind a tiny woman who must be close to eighty. She's trying to dump her trash when Felix strolls up. We watch the woman stand on her tiptoes; she takes three heaves but can't clear the lip of the disgusting steel box. Finally I step forward, smile, take the pink plastic garbage can from her, and dump it for her. She takes the can back, stares at me as if I were the village rapist, and marches off.

"She appreciated that," says Felix. "I can tell."

"It would seem so," I say and dump my trash.

Felix lights up another of those little cigars. "So?" he says.

"So what?" I answer.

"You decide?"

I set my trash can down and look into Felix's puffy face. "I think so."

He inhales; smoke curls out of his nostrils. "And?"

"I'm going to find him," I say, "if I can."

"Hmm." Felix looks around as a middle-aged woman comes up and dumps her garbage. She glances at Felix before walking away.

"Retired school teacher," Felix says. "Single."

I watch as the woman enters a ground-level apartment. "And?" I ask.

"She hit on me," Felix says. His smile is out of character.

"She looks nice," I say.

"Saw through me. Ina heartbeat."

I laugh.

"Got a nice dinner at her place out of it."

"Felix, you are incorrigible."

He shrugs. "So this guy, who is he?"

"Like I said, a man I worked for. Played a strong role in my life when I was a teenager and a young man. He meant a lot to me."

Felix drops his smoke and steps on it. "I been thinkin'. Wouldn't do it if I was you. Look this fella up, I mean. Loser of an idea."

"Felix, just because your teacher ended up in prison—"

"Nah, nah," he interrupts, "it's not that."

"What, then?"

"You can't go back, I tell ya. People, they get different on ya. They go all strange. 'Specially if yer down, they'll look the other way. It's embarrassing to 'em."

I think of Tommy calling me embarrassing and feel my face grow warm under Felix's admonition. I leave him standing at the Dumpster, go back to my apartment, and crank up Mr. Coffee; I make six cup's worth. The first cup is good; next one will be okay—it'll be downhill from there. I pull the drapes halfway open and stand coaxing coffee over the lip of the cup, and look out. I wouldn't have done this a week ago. Had no interest in anything beyond those putrid drapes. Now it boils down to this: who do you ask for advice when the question is about the very person you would have asked?

My father answers the phone on the third ring. His voice sounds older than last time. When would that have been, a year? I didn't talk to him when my marriage soured or when my job went away. Mom, I talked with her both times, so he knows everything from her.

"Hi, Dad," I say. "It's Edmund."

"Why, Edmund," he says, working on a bit of enthusiasm.

32

"This is a surprise."

"Yeah, it has been a while. How are things in Phoenix?" I ask.

"Nice, a little too warm today, but nice. It will be much hotter later, in the summer."

"But you have air conditioning, right?"

"Oh yes," he answers. "Can't live here without air conditioning. So how's the weather in Portland?"

"Typical springtime in the Northwest, you know. A little sun, rain, occasional sleet, more sun, and more rain. Off and on."

"I remember it well," he says. "Do you want to talk to your mother?"

The typical male handoff, a little small talk before giving the phone to the female of the house. Extended male conversations on the phone are a contradiction.

"Maybe later. I really called to talk to you," I say cautiously.

There is a pause before he says, "Is that right?"

"Yes. Do you have a few minutes?"

"Well…I don't…"

"I won't take long," I say, to ease his hesitancy.

"All right, Edmund, what is it?"

I turn away from the phone and clear my throat. "Uh, of course you are aware of my problems."

"Uh-huh." His voice is noncommittal.

"I mean, the divorce and then the company I worked for being sold—so I'm out there. You know all of that, right?"

I can hear him inhale. "Your mother keeps me apprised of everything happening with you and Sugar."

So that's a yes. "This is so strange. Here I am going to turn fifty this fall, and I'm calling my father for personal advice." I laugh nervously. My father doesn't respond to my disclaimer, so I plow on. "My situation for the last six months has been discouraging," I say, "to say the least."

"Uh-huh," my father responds.

"No marriage, no job, and, frankly, I slipped into a funk."

"A funk," my father echoes. "What's that?"

I try a small laugh. "Feeling low," I answer. "Feeling withdrawn. And, on top of that, I was very angry for a time."

My father's voice gets muffled; then I realize he's speaking to my mother. "It's Edmund, dear. We're…having a talk." Then he's back. "Yes, Edmund, I'm here. Ah, so this *funk* you call it, are you still in it?"

"Yes," I say. "That is, partly I am."

"Partly."

"Well, it's…I think it's not exactly something you can get over by drinking a glass of orange juice or taking a multivitamin."

There is another long pause before my father says, "What can you do? See a therapist or something?"

"No, I don't want to do that," I answer.

"I imagine not," my father says. "So, Edmund, what is it you want from me? You need money? We're on a fixed income, but I suppose…"

"No, Dad, that's not it." I take a deep breath. "Like I said, I want your advice on something." This has to be a shock for him because stubborn Edmund has never asked his parents for advice, ever.

"Is that right," my father says, sounding almost bewildered. He's in his early seventies and, out of the blue, his only son calls to ask for his help—a first.

"Yes."

"All right, what is it, Edmund?"

"I think I need to talk to someone," I say.

"I thought you didn't want to see—"

"Not a shrink, I mean, therapist. Someone else. Actually, this is Sugar's idea."

"Sugar," he says, brightening. Anything Sugar says or does has always carried more weight with my parents, especially my father. "Is that right? Her idea, then?"

34

"That's right. Sugar's idea is that I look up a person who was an important role model when I was young."

"A role model. I see. When you look up this person, as you say, then what?"

"Just talk with him, see if we can communicate like we did all those years ago."

"And this will get you out of this funk business?" my father asks.

"I don't know, Dad."

"Uh-huh." He hesitates then asks, "So what is it you want from me?"

"I want to know what you think of the idea?"

"I see," he says. "Can you tell me who this person is?"

"You'll probably remember his name," I say. "Richard Vickerman. I worked with him for many years first in grocery and then in the non-foods business, at the Bob-Buys Company, you may remember. I called him Dick Vic."

My father is so quiet that for a moment I think the line has gone dead. "Dad, you there?"

"Yes, I'm here," he says softly.

"So do you remember that name? Dick Vic?"

"Oh yes, I certainly do remember that name."

"Good," I say. "You see Richard, Dick Vic, was a real mentor to me and was someone I could talk with about things."

"Things?" my father asks. "What things?"

"Oh, kid stuff, about girls, problems in school—even getting along with you and Mom. Growing-up issues."

"I see, and you want to talk with this man again and see if it will help you get back on your feet. Is that it?"

"Something like that. What do you think, Dad? Should I do it?"

I heard him breathe in. "Let me tell you, Edmund. You may not have known this, but I was very aware of how much you looked up to that man, Mr. Vickerman. And I felt that in many ways his presence in your life supplanted mine. There were times when I felt like an outsider with my own son who never came to me with his problems or for advice about life. I resented what he had with you, and I was hurt because you went elsewhere for what I had hoped to give you from the day you were born."

I am in shock. Neither of us speaks for a very long moment. My throat constricts.

"Dad," I finally say, "I didn't know. I'm so very sorry."

His voice is breathy and nervous. "Thank you for calling. I've wanted to find a way to tell you that for years. I finally decided that I would go to my grave, and you would never know how I'd suffered. Now that you know, I don't feel any better and may have only hurt you in return. I'm sorry."

"Dad, I'm—"

"Edmund, go find this Dick Vic. Find him and talk to him. I hope he can help you find yourself again. I think Sugar has had another good idea. Now, I have no more to give to this. I am spent."

With that he disconnects, and I get the dial tone on my Princess phone.

-5-

I'm up. It's Friday morning and only eight o'clock. I can't believe it: already showered, shaved, and have a plan for the day. I haven't resolved the conversation with my father yesterday, but his revelation is maybe something he and I can use to dissolve years of distance between us. In spite of regrets for my father's pain, I've decided: I will look for Dick Vic. And now that I have decided, just what does that mean? Is there an obvious end point? I know one thing, I need to thank the man—I never did that. But I'm not kidding myself, mostly want to find out that if seeing him will be like it was: *Hear me out, Dick, then tell me what to do.* Then again, maybe there will be nothing to prove or to absolve. I can only know that by finding Richard Vickerman.

There is one egg in the fridge and a slice of bologna; I fry those up, enjoy a hearty breakfast with coffee while I thumb through the white pages of the Portland metro telephone directory. I find six listings under Vickerman and pencil them in a column onto the back of a junk-mail envelope. There is no Richard, no R. A., plain R., or Dick: three male names, one female, and two with just an initial. After reading the names a dozen times, I suds up a dishrag with a bar of Ivory soap, wash the breakfast plate, frying pan and the fork, put them in the drainer, pour another cup of coffee, lean against the counter, and look back at that envelope. I get the chills, the kind you get when the flu's coming on. Looking up those names and writing them down is the first intentional act I've taken in so long that it gives me the willies. I watch that envelope like it will do something on its own, and swallow coffee and keep staring; maybe that's enough for today—the list, names and numbers. Big step.

I sit on the couch in the dimness of my tiny living room. It is quiet. The envelope is still on the table, it's ten o'clock, and I've missed Martha Stewart. I retrieve the envelope and reread the names and numbers before sticking it under a Domino's Pizza rubber magnet on the refrigerator. I go take a pee. I come back; the list is right where I left it. I lift the Princess from the wall, put my finger on the envelope just below the first number for A. Vickerman, and dial. I swallow and lean my forehead against the coolness of the refrigerator door and listen to the repetitive tone. Three rings, four rings, I lick my lips just in case. On the fifth ring a perky female voice says "Hi," and I almost speak, but she goes on: "You've reached Alice, please leave a message, bye." When the tone sounds I start to hang up but decide what the hell.

"Yes," I start, clear my throat, and say, "My name is Edmund Kirby-Smi…Kirby, Edmund Kirby." To hell with Sylvia, I'm not a Smith anymore. "I'm trying to reach a *Richard* Vickerman. If you know him, please call me back. Thank you." I leave my number and hang up; my heart is beating as if I'd just made an obscene phone call.

I drink a glass of water from the tap and dial the next name, Adam Vickerman. A guy answers on the second ring, sounds old. "Nope, don't know any other Vickermans." No answer at D. Vickerman; voice mail for Ivan Vickerman—leave a message; the same for Joan Vickerman. Waldo Vickerman answers, booming out "Vickerman Properties!"

"Richard? Yeah, if he's the same one. We're related. Second cousins, I think, maybe third. Who knows?" He laughs a

38

salesman's laugh. "Wish I could help you, but I don't have a clue where he is or *if* he is—alive I mean." Laughs again. "Must be what? In his seventies, mid-to late seventies. Last time I saw him I was maybe twenty. That was at least twenty-five years ago. Wow, a quarter century, how 'bout that?"

"Any other relatives who might know?" I ask.

"Nope, not from our end. You know how it is—two, three generations out no one keeps track like the old days. As I recall old Dick, he only had but one child, a girl. I can see her in my head but can't bring up her name, probably married anyway. Not a Vickerman by now, likely."

I check Waldo off my list and make a grocery run—catch the bus and ride to Safeway. I can shop for a month in fifteen minutes: frozen dinners, soup, packaged macaroni-and-cheese dinners, ramen noodles, beer, wine, bologna, cheese, canned vegetables, toilet paper—slam-bam. Have them double-bag everything, and I'm back in the apartment in less than an hour. The phone is ringing when I struggle through the door with four bulging sacks. It's a woman responding to my first call, Alice Vickerman. She sounds young and suspiciously curious. "Who is Richard Vickerman and who are you?" she asks. I check her off the list and put away my stores. Four to go. I watch M*A*S*H reruns every night, so naturally I'm just getting comfortable and into the story when the phone rings for number three. Ivan Vickerman just moved here from Illinois and has no local relation "Thank God," says he. I just get my head back on the pillow when Joan Vickerman calls. She is an anxious woman, is Joan, wants desperately to be of help, racks her brain, and sends up test balloons of possible sources: the Internet, city directory. All stuff I'd have to go to the library for—I'll try that if nothing else works. The theme music is thrumming when I get back to M*A*S*H, so I go toss a frozen entrée into the oven and check Ivan and Joan off, noting that only D. Vickerman remains. What the hell, I dial up D. and get a pickup on the second ring. A woman listens to my query and then evidently hands the phone off to her bodyguard.

"Who is this?" The voice is two octaves lower than dirt.

I explain my quest again.

"Ain't no *Richard* Vickerman here. Don't call here again." What, and join in on the fun you folks must be having? Heartbreak.

The beef stroganoff concoction tastes pretty good. Even found a few chunks of meat in the white cream sauce and a hint of onion and an occasional slice of mushroom to boot—living the good life. I draw a fat black line through D. Vickerman as I eat and look at my nowhere list and wonder if that's it. What can I do next? I can't make up my mind, so I decide to watch *Law and Order*.

It comes to me about the time they find the body of a woman jogger in Central Park. I roll off the bed and stiff-leg barefoot into the kitchen and pull out the telephone directory for the second time in six months and begin thumbing: Thorson, Tindall, Tolliver. Damn, there he is: Wm. T. Tolliver. Bud Tolliver, salesman extraordinaire, still kicking. I've known Bud Tolliver forever—back to when I was a high school kid bagging groceries and stocking shelves at Gilson's Superette. Bud was peddling pasta products in those days. Young man, black wavy hair, sharp nose—had this funny laugh like a hiccup. And he was always kind to me, never too big to give some time to a geeky kid. He was a ladies man, too, and loved his highballs.

I remember Bud called old man Gilson in the middle of the night once, drunk, in jail, needing bail. Gilson, the mean s.o.b., was a teetotaler, squeaky religious, always closed on Sundays even though it cost him, and wouldn't hear of paying to bail a sinner out of jail. Next day Bud came in, making his usual sales call, apologized all to hell to the old man. Gilson nodded and must have felt guilty over leaving this fine young man in jail because he gave Tolliver an order for a hundred cases of pasta products.

Dick Vic had two end displays of Colleti spaghetti, egg noodles, and elbow macaroni for six months trying to clear that deal and old man Gilson's conscience.

A woman answers my call cheerily and asks me to wait a moment. I wonder if she had been one of Bud's host of adoring females, the one to make the final cut. I can hear her calling his name, saying she didn't know who it was, a man, for him. Suddenly someone's breathing in my earpiece, and the voice that had made me smile so many times is saying "Yes" in a voice made strong from years of selling with enthusiasm.

"I'm calling with this great deal on Colleti spaghetti," I say.

Silence on the line. I imagine a smile coming onto old Bud's face like always, even if he'd been tricked. "Who the hell is this? Can't be…no…is that you, Reynolds?"

"Nope."

"Colleti, that's ancient history," Bud says. "Everybody's dead I can think of. Ain't feeling so chipper myself." He laughs. "Okay, I give."

"Edmund Kirby."

"Edmund!" He shouts into my ear. "Which one of us is still alive?"

"Guess it's you," I say, "because I'm calling from the grave." If he only knew.

"That's the echo I hear." Same old Bud. "How the hell are you, and why you calling an old man? And still ragging me about that Colleti deal."

"Me? I'd never do that."

He laughs. "So why am I being honored with this call?"

"I have a question for you," I say. "About Dick Vic."

"Dick Vic," he says slow, drawing the name out. "Just when I can't find my car keys this guy calls and asks me something I *can* remember. Geez Louise, haven't thought of Vickerman in zillions. How the hell is he?"

"Wish I knew. That's why I'm calling, trying to locate him. I thought maybe you'd have some ideas. Been through the phone directory, no luck."

"I hear you. His wife, Dottie, she's dead, long time now. There was the daughter, Anne, Angie…"

"Andrea, isn't it?" I suddenly remember, the pretty girl with braces, the one I had a crush on.

"That's it. Andrea. Tried her? Wait, she married some guy. Wouldn't be Vickerman anymore. Divorced, too, come to think of it."

He's filtering the past, fussing and tumbling his memory and talking himself into a possibility. Says he knows a fellow, another old salesman, warhorse who might have an idea of how to get in touch with the daughter. Nothing certain, but he promises to call me the next day, then blends right in to his salesman's probe.

"Dick Vic," he says, "one of the good guys. So what's up? You owe him money?"

"Probably" I laugh. "Nah, just had an urge to look him up. You know." I feel heat in my face knowing Bud's going ask what I'm doing but not wanting him to do that. He does it anyway.

"Sure, sure. Say, you still with Singleton's? That was it, wasn't it?"

"Yep, but nope. Not for a spell." I pause. "Truth is, I'm in between."

Bud laughs like yesteryear and says, "Lotta that going around." Always give a guy an out.

He promises to do some checking and get back to me, which he does while I'm toweling off from my second shower in two days the very next morning.

"Hey, Bud, that was quick."

"Yeah, well, you know me. Just open the gate and pat me on the butt. Anyway, I found her."

I cinch the bath towel around my waist. "Really?" I feel a twinge of uncertainty.

"Yep. Called Bill Twixell. Remember him? Nabisco salesman? Twixell and Dick Vic, they were big golf buddies. Anyhow, he remembered her married name. Goes by Andrea Hewitt, still lives here in Portland. Guess she's divorced now."

"Thanks. I really appreciate this."

"My pleasure," Bud says. He gives me her address and phone number, and we promise to keep in touch.

-6-

I'm looking at Andrea Hewitt's phone number one more time, drinking my third cup of coffee—it's nine-thirty, Saturday morning. I have on some halfway decent clothes just in case this thing works out: my best pair of khakis (too tight), a yellow polo shirt with an irreversible wine stain just low enough that I can tuck it in, and a pair of tasseled loafers. I take in a couple of deep breaths to settle the feathers floating in my stomach, hold the Princess in my palm, and punch the numbers. I lean on the counter and moisten my lips.

I've been rebuilding a mental image of Dick Vic's daughter as I remember her. Andrea's maybe three or four years younger than I am. She used to drop by Gilson's to see her dad; I was probably eighteen or so at the time. She was pretty, had blonde hair and spectacular blue eyes. I was dating Sylvia by that time, but still I harbored a secret infatuation for Andrea Vickerman. We used to exchange looks and smiles—knowing glances, those exciting awkward moments of youthful attraction.

There's a click in my ear after three rings; I rise up off my elbows as low-voltage fingers run up my neck. The voice isn't that of the young female in my head but one with the timbre of maturity. I hesitate maybe two heartbeats after the voice grants access, trying to imagine what Richard Vickerman's daughter should sound like: tone, cadence, enunciation? She's saying hello for the third time.

"Uh yes," I stammer. "Is this Andrea...Andrea Hewitt?"

"That's me," she answers. "Who's this?"

"You may not remember me, but my name is Edmund Kirby."

"I don't...oh, Edmund Kirby!" she almost shouts my name. "Edmund. Of course I remember. My word, how are you?"

"Okay."

"What a surprise," she chirps. "How long has it been? Let's see, I'll bet it's been what, fifteen...no closer to—twenty years? Can it be?"

"Yeah," I say and cough out a little laugh. "Think that's about right."

"That's amazing. So, Edmund, how are you?" she asks again. "Wait, I've already asked that. Okay how about, to what do I owe the honor of your call?"

No warm lead-in, I just spit it out: "To find out where your dad is."

Silence. I press the phone tighter to my head and hear a faint but high-pitched sigh. We agree to meet.

I've learned the fundamentals of public transportation in the past few months, so I know it will take me under an hour to get into the city from North Portland. I leave almost as soon as Andrea hangs up, walk up to North Lombard and catch the TriMet bus #44 and am in the city in less than fifty minutes, transfer and all. I'm nursing an Americano when I see a woman I assume to be Andrea approach the front door of the shop. She picked this place, a cramped coffeehouse on First Avenue a block or so from the Willamette riverfront. The place is called Java-Jinks. I like it. It's cozy, worn around the edges—I fit right in.

This woman I think is Andrea is fighting to get the door open while wrestling a purse that hangs precariously by a thin shoulder strap. By the time I decide that it is her and push up out of my chair to help, she has gone into this spinning motion, frees herself, takes off her sunglasses, and looks around. I raise a hand and offer her a smile; she nods, swings the purse back, and weaves her way over between tables and chairs. I can see nothing that reminds me of her father or of the girl she used to be. She is not lean, has none of Dick Vic's angularity of face or his coloring. She is pleasant looking, full-faced, fair-skinned, has shortish blonde hair, and is carrying an extra pound or two. Her large blue eyes are the only part that looks familiar, and they are focused on me, wide and searching.

I can imagine I must be a shock to her. She is plumpish, but I am flat-out fat, filled out way beyond her memory of me. I'm sure of that. My receding hair is long overdue for a shearing: hairy neck and tangles over my ears. I've combed it back as best I can, but with little improvement. Back when she knew me I was a fit, wiry young guy, always running—never walked, always ran. Had thick hair. Like I said, we noticed each other, but I doubt that she'll remember those moments of infatuation. I've likely killed off any such sweet memories for her in one stroke. It's one thing to lie around like a cadaver in your own space; it's another to come out of hiding in front of people who knew you as a productive and responsible, even a once appealing, person.

Her smile is cautious. "Edmund?" The eyes confirm the doubt in her voice.

I raise my arms. "The one and only." We both chuckle while she settles into a chair.

"Well," she says, looking around, "this place used to be really nice."

"I like it," I say, "the knockabout patina, the mismatched cups. I fit right in."

She smiles and sticks her sunglasses up in her hair. "Yes, well, Edmund, what a total surprise to get your phone call. It was so good to hear from you after all these years. Time flies, doesn't it?"

I give her a grin and wonder how many more clichés she'll dish out. "That it does," I retort, joining in. "Can I get you something? Coffee? Tea, maybe?" She wants a mocha, I another Americano; I pay for them like I have a financial base. We sit and sip and dip into times past—back when everything was yet to come. Then we slide into our grown-up past and talk about marriages, children, divorce. The what-came-next part, we aren't going there yet.

She is enjoying her second mocha, again at my expense, before she brings up her father. "Edmund, I have to tell you that Daddy and I, we haven't spoken for a long time. We're not on good terms, to put it mildly. He cut me out of his life seven years ago, just after my thirty-ninth birthday." She looks into her cup and licks chocolate off her lip. "Or maybe I cut him out of mine."

"Sounds like a toss-up," I offer.

"Yes, well." She reaches into her purse and brings out a hankie and blows her nose. "Like they say, life happens. Daddy's been out of my life so long I sometimes forget."

"No contact at all?" I ask.

She shakes her head. "No. Sad, really. Sometimes families hurt one another beyond repair."

"That's true," I say, thinking *Just ask me.* "What happened?"

Andrea studies my unfamiliar face. Man, those blue eyes are still impressive.

"Mom got sick," she says. "Real sick. Cancer. That was over ten years ago. Rocked Daddy right to his soul. His Dottie, his life-long soul mate, was *not* going to die. Wouldn't hear of it. So they fought it. I should say Daddy fought it. Mom, she knew. She heard the doctors and knew the truth." She blows her nose again. "I'll always believe that Mom wouldn't have suffered like she did those last two years if they hadn't gone ahead with all that stuff:

the chemo, radiation, all of it. God, she practically glowed in the dark. You know what they say about cancer treatment? First they kill you. Then try and bring you back from the dead.

"The last two months were awful. Daddy insisted on her coming home from the hospital, so he could take care of her. He didn't use hospice. That would have been giving up." She dabs at her eyes. "When she died, I felt so relieved that her pain was over. That's where I made my mistake—at a gathering after the funeral I said I was glad it was over. And that I wished she hadn't had to suffer so long." She leans toward me, and her eyes fill again. "Edmund, I was choking with grief and made the mistake of saying that we shouldn't have put Mom through the torture of all that stuff, all that toxic junk." She slumps back. "I haven't had one word with my dad since that afternoon."

"You tried to make contact?"

She shrugs. "At first. But now I don't know where he is. Three months after she died, Daddy suddenly put the house on the market and vanished. I've tried to find him, but not in the last couple of years. He could be anywhere."

"Do you want to find him?" I ask.

"What's this about, Edmund? Why are you wanting to see him again? After all this time."

I'm sitting with a stranger. She's sitting with a stranger. I'm looking at this woman I don't recognize; except for her eyes she's just someone I'm sharing a table and a cup of coffee with. And I'm assuming she is thinking: *I drove all the way into the city for this?* The fine lines of her emerging crow's feet crimp down while she waits for me to unveil my conspiratorial intent. I can tell that I'm making her anxious by the way she is holding her mouth. It's a nice mouth, painted a rosy shade, but her lips are tense even when she smiles. And I'm puckering my own mouth, deciding how to explain why I want to see her father. That I just need to see him again and tell him of my pain, like

I used to. To tell him *Thank you* and ask him to do it again—tell me what to do. Help me figure things out just like we did in Gilson's back room.

"No big deal," I begin with a lie. She squints at that. "Just, you know, I haven't seen him in so long. Just came to me, that's all."

Andrea lifts her cup and drains the cold remains but keeps looking at me over the rim. Dubious. "You went to some effort to find me for no big deal. I'm unlisted. I have a different last name."

"Uh-huh." I nod.

"How did you, anyway? Find me?"

"I started off dialing every Vickerman in the phone book. It was a blind alley, of course. Of course I didn't know if your dad was living in Mexico, Las Vegas, or even if he was...alive. Sorry."

She merely blinks at my boorish reference to death.

"I just kept ticking off possibilities and lucked into calling a sales rep I know from years ago. You remember Bud Tolliver?"

She shakes her head and reaches up to keep her sunglasses from falling out of her hair. "Daddy rattled off names of people," she says, "you know, store talk. I don't remember much of it."

"I can imagine," I say. "Anyway, Bud, this rep, he knew a guy who had your married last name, and here we are."

"Must have been Bill Twixell," she says.

"That's the one."

We both look up as a young man decked out in iridescent red spandex bangs into the shop and parks his road bike against the wall. "But I'm a dead end," she's saying while watching tight glutei walk by. "What now?" she asks.

"You really don't know where he is, then?" She shakes her head and reaches up to protect her sunglasses. "Wouldn't be protecting his whereabouts, would you?"

Her laugh is brittle. "Look," she says, "if I had any idea where the old coot was, I'd be in his face telling him…" She stops and blinks; tears come. She wipes her eyes with a napkin and tries to laugh. "Real tough, aren't I?"

"Sorry," I say. "I didn't mean to stir up the past."

She inhales. "Maybe it needs stirring up."

"I lost track of your dad after I left Bob-Buys. I always meant to keep in touch. I just didn't—that's a big regret. What did he do, stay on at Bob-Buys?"

"Yeah," she says, "he stayed right there, retired from Bob-Buys, back in, let's see, he'd be seventy-two now, so, do the math, he retired in 1993. That's right, '93. Stayed on as long as he could to keep his health insurance for Mom and for his retirement. He hated it there the last years. They demoted him, I think. He retired two weeks after Mom died."

"You know, I had a crush on you," I say. "When I was working at Gilson's with your dad."

Andrea blinks at my sudden change of subject; I see a bit of color in her face. "I kind of remember something like that," she says. "I vaguely remember having some hot boy-girl eye contact with this young man when I'd come into the store. Was that you?" she chides.

"You know it was. I would hang around waiting for you to smile and blink those blue eyes my way."

Andrea looks up as a woman passes, juggling a cardboard tray of scones and paper coffee cups. "As I recall," she says, "you had a steady girl when you were doing all this flirting. Whatever happened with that?"

"Sylvia. I married her," I say. "A hurry-up event it was, too."

She laughs. "Oh, one of those."

"Yep. Lasted through twenty-seven years and two kids. That was as long as Sylvia could handle."

"Divorce?"

"Uh-huh, six months ago."

"Join the club," she says and smiles sympathetically. "Fifteen years for me. Mine's been over for two years."

I raise my cup. "A toast to…to what?" I laugh.

"Surviving," she says.

We empty our cups of cold coffee, and I wonder if I would be surviving.

"So, Edmund, what are you doing now?" She asks the question cautiously.

There it is, the irresistible question—the one designed to cut away the mystery surrounding a person who has been absent and is now a curiosity. Her eyes are widening, intensifying the question.

"Nothing." I say it so easily I surprise myself.

"Oh." She blinks. "You've retired? No, you're too young for that."

"No, not retired."

Her laugh is uncertain. "Okay." She studies me, her head titled. "Vacation?"

"I'd call it suspended animation."

She raises her eyebrows. "That's a new one. So you're not working, but you're not retired or on vacation of any kind," she goes on. "I'm not sure…"

"You want the whole story or a summary?" I say.

"Start with the summary."

I take in a slow breath, look across the coffee shop, and begin. "Divorce, kid dysfunction, job loss, financial meltdown, rage, loss of direction, lethargy, kick-in-the-butt—now you." When I look back, her expression is one of sadness warmed by some measure of sympathy.

"Who kicked you in the butt?" she asks.

"My little sister, Sugar. She's been on my ass for months."

"Sugar?" I nod. "She got you going, then?"

51

"No," I say. "I resisted her pestering. It drove me underground. Finally, after she'd exhausted her reproaches, she just said I ought to talk to someone."

"Like a therapist?"

I nod. "But I wouldn't ever do that. Then she happened to mention your dad."

"Really? How come?"

"Who knows? Sugar was just throwing ideas against my head. She doesn't know that that one projectile had the germ of possibility."

Andrea takes her sunglasses off her head and sets them on the table. "And what has this to do with my father?"

"We used to sit in the back room at Gilson's after hours, your dad and I, and he would listen to my woes. You know, the kind that plagues a teenage boy: problems that your parents would never understand, a world crisis pretty much every week. Those kind?"

She just looks at me.

"Anyway, he listened to me and would help me decipher each crisis that was sure to ruin my life." I laugh; she doesn't.

"Strange," she says, "he never listened to me much, and— believe me—I had my share of life-ending dramas."

"Who did you talk to?" I ask.

She smiles. "Lucy Downs. My closest friend in all the world back then. I haven't thought of her in years. But Lucy was my listening post, and I hers. We shared the most intimate details of our superficial lives."

"Guys don't do that," I say. "Not our fears, being liked or not liked, or gut-level problems with parents or being dumped by a girl. We'd talk bravado but not the stuff inside. I didn't have a friend like Lucy."

Andrea is quiet then says, "Those were our kid days, Edmund. To grow up we had to go through those childish pains, but that was then. Do you think my dad can talk to you again like you are a boy?"

I feel my face warm. "It went beyond that, Andrea. Dick was around, in my life, until my early twenties."

"But still."

"Look," I say. "I just want to see him. Will you help me or not?"

She looks at me, and I can sense her measuring me. "I don't know where he is, like I said."

"But you want to see him again, don't you?" She doesn't respond. "Well, don't you?" I repeat.

We sit, neither speaking. The coffee shop ebbs and flows about us, and we each are processing our own thoughts. Andrea looks at her watch. I assume that is a sign that this is over, but then she leans back and seems to settle in. The hiss of the espresso machine continues like an old steam engine idling at the railroad station, bleeding off surplus energy.

"Maybe I do," she says all of a sudden, "want to find him."

I keep my mouth shut for once.

"But…part of me is afraid to."

"Maybe we can help each other," I say.

She fiddles with a silver bracelet on her right arm. "I'm not sure how I feel about you, Edmund…and what you want from him."

"I won't hurt him," I say. "He meant a lot to me…that's all."

She gathers herself and her purse and her sunglasses and gets up from the table.

"Let me think about it," she says. "Give me your phone number. I'll call you, okay?"

I nod, scribble my number on a piece of napkin and hand it to her. She pauses at the door of the coffee shop and looks back at me; her expression is one of perplexed sympathy.

Will we find Richard Vickerman? Everything depends on whether Andrea sees me as a lunatic or not. Before catching the bus back home, I wander down to the riverfront and stroll along the sea wall. The Willamette River is alive with spring power boaters, and the Japanese cherry trees are in full bloom at the north end of Waterfront Park. The bikers and joggers and walkers are out in big numbers. Everyone, save the homeless guys sleeping on the grass in the sun, seems to have somewhere to be. Maybe I will feel that way soon. Who knows?

I catch the bus at Fourth and Oak and head back to the beehive.

-7-

I don't know what I expect from Andrea. If she's smart, she won't call this guy from her distant past claiming he needs to see her father so he can revisit his youth because his life is in the crapper. It's already Wednesday, been four days, and I haven't heard a word. While waiting her out I have managed to wash a load of clothes and change the sheets on my bed—well ahead of schedule. I've also used the time to delve more into my grandfather's stamp album; I especially like United States Commemoratives. I'm eating a bowl of ramen noodles with the album open to stamps issued in 1934 featuring national parks. I'm looking at an uncancelled 4¢ stamp of the Mesa Verde National Park when Andrea calls.

"I found him," she says, excited. "Well, almost found him."

"You did? Where is he?"

"Edmund," she hesitates, "I've been thinking this over, and I'm not sure I ought to do this."

"Do what? Find your dad?"

"Let you get involved."

"So why'd you call me, then?"

Her laugh is nervous. "I don't know. Crazy, isn't it?"

"I'd say so. So how did you find him?" I change the subject.

She laughs some more. "You'll never believe this. I just

called Bob-Buys and got hold of a woman I know who worked there when Dad did. She works in human resources. I whined a lot."

"Can't believe it," I say. "The HR people I knew were tight-fisted as hell with employee records."

"When I mentioned that Daddy's been missing and I'm trying to find him after years and years…anyway, she was in near tears."

"You are bad."

"I know. But she bent the rules, and now I owe her lunch."

"So, what did you find out?"

"I thought I could get Dad's address because of his pension check. The thing is, a couple of years ago everything went to a direct deposit system instead of mailing out checks."

"So?"

"She gave me an address, but I don't know if he's still there."

"Bet he is," I say. "Old folks don't move around much."

"Edmund, I don't want him hurt. I know I said I was upset with him, but he is my dad. I guess I've saved some space for him after all. He was a good man. Wasn't he? Mostly?"

"He was," I agree. "Of course he was. Why else would I be doing this?"

She pauses. "Yes, I know what you said, but…"

"If you think I'm crazy or something, why tell me where he is?"

For a moment I think she has hung up, but at that instant she says, "Because I want to know if he's okay. Safe and well…and, you know, okay."

"Do it yourself, then," I say.

"I can't." She sighs. "I…well, I just can't."

I laugh. "Aren't we a pair? You think I'm nuts, and I think you're balmy." I wait a beat and ask, "You want to go with me? To find him?"

She inhales then breathes her answer into my ear. "Not this time. Maybe after...after you find him."

"You mean IF I find him. I've never been a sleuth before."

We both laugh before she cautiously reads off a street address in Banks, a small town west of Portland, on the way to the coast off the Wilson River Highway. After imagining Richard Vickerman hiding out in some far-off place, to have him but a few miles away gives me goose bumps. Andrea and I kick some *Wells* and *Okay thens* back and forth before she whispers a plea to let her know what I find out and hangs up.

I sit here looking at an address on a Turner Street in Banks, Oregon, and swallow against a sudden sense of anticipation. So, what now?

I venture out. It's raining, one of those spring drenchers. Instead of going back to get my broken-down umbrella, I suck in a breath and lope across the compound as fast as my conditioning allows. I arrive at Felix's front door panting, seeing spots, and drenched from my Motorcraft logo tee shirt to my rubber thongs. Eventually Felix responds to my banging and looks me up and down, holding his burning cigarillo in one hand up and away from my wetness.

"It's raining," I say.

Felix looks over his shoulder out the window. Damned if the sun isn't out.

"Well it was, buckets."

He walks away and leaves the door open, tosses me the towel hanging from the fridge door handle, and goes and stands in front of the television. A soap opera is on. Felix stands there smoking and watching until a commercial comes on, hits the mute button on the remote, and shakes his head.

"Bastard," he says, "knew he'd do that."

I'm toweling my head. I'm not into that particular soap, but I'm close with one on another channel. So I know where the guy's coming from. There's always a scoundrel, and there's always a bitch.

"Could turn it off," I say. "Pick it up tomorrow. Be the same."

Felix sucks on his smoke, squints at me, holds the remote up high, and hits the kill button. The screen goes black. He throws the remote onto the couch, goes to the fridge, and holds out an X-brand beer. I nod; he throws it at me. I catch it in one hand and pull the tab and take a swig. That's our male bonding.

We go out onto his balcony and sit and drink and watch the sidewalk steam after the rain I swear really happened. I point out the sweating concrete to Felix, and he shrugs. Truth prevails. I finish the beer and go get another—don't want to rush this.

"You still have that car?" I ask him after the second beer.

A very long moment later, he turns his head and studies me. "Nice hair." I reach up and touch the eggbeater effect of my toweling.

"Do you?" I lick my fingertips and try to pat the errant strands into place. "Still have that car?"

He sucks from the can and looks pensive. "Nineteen-seventy Chevrolet Chevelle Super Sport, 396 cubes, 350 horse, turbo tranny. Red with white stripes and hood scoop. Yeah, I still got it. It's under that blue tarp in the parking lot. You've seen it out there, far corner."

"Yes. Does it run?"

"Think so. Leastwise I start 'er up once a month—on the first, if I remember. Maybe longer'n that this last time. Quit driving it regular quite a while back. Only take her out when she's running low on start-up gas. Gettin' an automobile is like marrying up with a gorgeous babe. After the sex, you're still married. Same with a car. After those first horny drives, you're still on the hook: insurance, monthly payments, repairs, gas. When you buy a car, yer tricked into thinking you made this investment, except the damn thing depreciates into nothingness before you know it. Suppose it'll run. It did when I shut it off that last time. Why?"

I sit up and shrug the damp shirt loose from my back. "I have to find someone," I answer.

"You mean that fella you was talking about?"

"Yes, I've decided to find him."

"Hmm." Felix looks down and nods. "Guess my little talk at the garbage bin wasn't convincing enough."

"I appreciate your advice," I say, "but I have to do this."

Felix digs through a drawer of stuff in the kitchen until he finds two keys on a ring with a Quaker State Oil tag attached to it and tosses them to me. "No insurance on it."

"That's okay. My license has expired anyway. I'll drive carefully."

"Whatever. This is it, then?"

"I think so."

"Been there. Hope this person's not no Stoddard."

"Me too."

Felix actually comes out to see me off this morning, a sunny Monday. The car looks pretty good. I've washed it, and the red paint is surprisingly bright considering the car's shrouded hibernation. Felix stands in the parking lot, hands in his pockets, his face flat and expressionless, and watches me drive away. I kill the engine, restart it, and give a wave that is not returned. Damn, the Chevelle has so much power that I spin the tires and fishtail pulling away from a stop sign. I fill up at the first gas station I come to, clean the windshield, and aim the car out Lombard. Then I catch the ramp onto I-5 and jump off onto the Fremont Bridge and take Highway 26 through the Vista Ridge tunnel. It's like taking that first drag after being off smokes for a long time; I'm feeling spacey, but the old driving skills are still there.

Out Highway 26, I'm holding my speed to just under fifty-five. The sun is out, and the Tualatin Valley is sparkling with its open fields and plots of nursery stock. There's something to be said for getting out. The fields lie out smooth and green, and far off the coast range etches its meandering silhouette against the sky. I feel like I'm driving back in time, in this old muscle car, heading west to revisit a person I knew back when I was a young man.

At Highway 6, I take the Tillamook exit and a couple of miles later pull off into Banks. The young woman who is selling me a vanilla latte from an espresso trailer tells me generally where Turner Street is. "It's not a very big town," she explains.

Two teenage boys give me a yell and stick their thumbs up as I pass the high school—they dig the Chevelle. I give the horn a sharp tap and keep driving. But I run out of town before I realize that I somehow missed the street. Doubling back, I end up with a big Ford pickup following me up close. So I quickly eyeball street signs, trying to make them out as they come at me: Market Street, Depot Street—pickup is right on my bumper—Sunset Avenue, damn—okay there it is, Turner.

I stab the brakes, make a sharp left turn, and the guy in the pickup practically climbs into my trunk. He lays on the horn as I slip off the main drag and slow down, entering a street of long-enduring, sad houses. Cruising slowly, looking side-to-side, I find number 311 toward the end of the street and pull up to the curb, leaving the engine running. It is a lonely little bungalow with splotchy blue weathered paint over tired shake siding and a tacked-on front porch fronted by a scruffy uncut lawn.

I turn off the ignition; the big engine calms. This house isn't what I'd expected Richard Vickerman to be living in. I can't really describe what I thought his house would look like, but this isn't it. I get out of the car, close the door with a click, and stare at the dreary place; it almost makes my dumpy apartment seem upper class. The blinds are pulled down tight as if from embarrassment.

When I move toward the front door, the crumbling front walk crunches like I'm treading on a bed of potato chips. I press the doorbell, but there is no response, so I knock several times. A mailbox attached to the porch wall has a clump of mail protruding from it. When no one answers the door, I look over my shoulder and, seeing no one, riffle through the mail—nothing but flyers and junk mail. The name on most of it is *Occupant*; but two envelopes, one a credit card come-on, the other from a company offering health insurance for seniors, are addressed to *Richard Vickerman*. I have the right address.

A quick trip around the building gets me nothing. I can't see in, and there's not a sign of life. Figuring that Richard must just be out, I sit in the car and decide to wait for him. After about half an hour a man comes out of a house across the street and gets into a green Toyota pickup. He backs out, looks at me for a moment, and then drives off. When he sees that I'm still there when he comes back fifteen minutes later, he ambles over and comes around to my open window.

"Ain't nobody home there, you know," he says.

I look up and smile. He is a big man, maybe forty, two days of beard at least; and he isn't pleased that I'm camped out across from his place. "Yeah, I know," I say all cheery like. "Just waiting for someone who lives there."

"Nobody livin' there," the man says. "It's empty."

"Is that so? Where did they go?"

"No idea, fella." The man looks toward the house. "But they ain't here now."

When I open the door and step out, the man doesn't move back; we're almost chest to chest. He's bigger than me, even in my inflated status. I smile and step to the side.

"I'm looking for a Richard Vickerman," I say. "You know him?"

He folds his arms and looks past me. "That the fella you think was living there?"

"Yes."

"How you know that?"

"Well," I laugh, "it was the address given to me for him, and there is mail in the box with his name on it."

The man's eyebrows go up. "You looked in that mailbox?"

"I did."

"Federal offense to mess with the mails."

"Look, Richard Vickerman is a close friend, and I've been looking for him. This is as close as I've been in a long time. Did you know him?" I ask again.

"Never met the man. Saw an older fella come and go over here, never traded a word with him. But he ain't here now."

"When did he leave?" I ask.

"Couldn't say," the man says. "Now, I just think you ought to move on. We don't much like people hanging around this street who don't live here. Even if you are driving this fancy car."

"You like this car?" I ask. "It's a 1970 Chevelle."

"It's okay." He clears his throat loudly and spits out into the yard of 311 Turner. "Like I say, best you move on. If not, I'll make a call to the cops."

The man walks across the street and stares at me when he gets to his front door; I stare back until he gives up and goes inside. Since it seems pretty likely that the guy might just call the police, I crank up the Chevelle and motor on out of Turner Street.

I'll be back.

-8-

The phone is ringing when I walk into my apartment carrying a bucket of KFC chicken, my reward to myself for being back out in the world and mixing it up. I catch the Princess on her fourth ring; it's Andrea.

"Yeah, I found the house," I say, "but not him."

"He wasn't home?"

"*No* one is living at 311 Turner Street. It's empty, and Richard… your dad has moved out, or so it appears."

"What do you mean *appears?*"

"Because a man who considers himself the sergeant-at-arms for Turner Street told me so. Just before he suggested that I move on."

"Do you really think Daddy was living there?"

"I found some old mail with his name on it, so yeah, he was there. Don't know how long he's been gone yet."

"Oh, my gosh," she says. "This is so strange, looking for him like this. So what do we do now?"

"Get a night's rest and go back. I'm not giving up. Just need to find someone out on Turner Street who will talk to me—not Attila the Hun who rousted me today. Want to go with me?"

A pause. "No," she says, "I can't. For one thing, I'm really busy right now. I have three closings tomorrow."

"Closings?"

"I sell real estate. Guess I didn't tell you how I feed myself. Well, anyway, things are booming. Besides I'm not up to snooping around after my father."

"I thought you wanted to see him."

"Well yeah, but…"

"So you want me to do the dirty work, is that it?"

She laughs. "I guess I do. Is that okay? I mean, you were going to do it anyway."

"I'll let you know if I can get a lead on where he might have gone," I say.

She sighs, and I promise to call tomorrow.

I am enjoying a drumstick of Kentucky Fried's original recipe, trying to keep from transferring grease to the stamp album, when someone knocks at the door. It's Felix. He stands in the doorway looking out of place.

"Well, well," I say. "The mount comes to the flat lands." I move back, and he walks in, stands with his hands in his pockets, and looks around.

"Dead ringer for my place," he says.

"You said that last time you graced my abode here."

"Just backwards is all," he continues. "See you're dining in."

"That's right, me and the Colonel. Want to share a thigh?"

"Don't mind if I do. Got anything to wash it down with?"

He's looking at the stamp album when I bring back a plate, paper towels, and two bottles of beer. He reaches into the chicken bucket and pulls out a piece of dark meat.

"You a stamp collector?"

"My grandfather was," I answer. "This was his collection. I just enjoy looking at them, relaxes me. I especially like the old U. S. Commemoratives. See this one, *The Immortal Chaplains*, issued in 1948, when you could mail a letter for three cents? Commemorates four chaplains who died in World War II when a torpedo hit the transport ship they were on in 1943. They gave up their own life jackets because there weren't enough to go around."

Felix bites down on thigh meat, looking all the time at the stamps. "Uh-huh. I used to collect stamps," he says. "Foreign ones. Bought a whole bag of 'em once. There was this 'Stamps of the World' ad in the back of a Batman comic book. I sent it in with three dollars." He laughs and wipes his fingers on the paper towel. "Pasted the damn things onto three-hole notebook paper with LePage's glue. Didn't know what the hell I was doing. Shoulda used them little paper hinges, you know...yeah, like them there. Tell you though, those stamps never ever came loose."

I close the album and slide it away from greasy fingers. "You just out slumming, or is there a reason for this call?" I ask.

"Just wondering how the car made out for you."

"Fine, ran great. Even got some appreciative hoots out of some high school boys."

Felix is nodding. "Kids, they love horsepower, bright paint, and chrome." He burps and wipes his mouth. "Best you put that tarp back on her when she's parked, though. Don't want to invite thieves and vandals."

"Sure," I say. "I should have thought of that. I'll go do it right now."

He raises a hand. "Later'll be okay." He reaches for another piece of chicken. "So, you find yer guy?"

"I found where he *used* to be. House was empty. I don't know where he is now."

"Where'd he used to be?"

"In Banks."

"You mean the town, Banks? That little spit of a place? I'll be damned. So a dead end. This mean it's over and done?"

"No, I'm going back out there tomorrow and start some real sleuthing. I'll find him."

Felix sets a cleaned-off chicken bone on his plate and picks up his beer. "Man, you making my teeth ache with all this activity. Maybe you ought to take the day off and come sit on my balcony. Watch the grass grow and see Miss Lolita walk the walk."

I shake my head. "I have the scent now, Felix. I'm going back out there and follow my nose."

"Hmm." He takes a pull from the bottle. "You in this for the thrill of the hunt now, or you still wanting to find this guy and face up to him?"

I start to clear the table of the KFC debris. "No, finding Richard is still something I have to do. Sort of a contract I've written up here." I tap the side of my head. "I owe him."

Felix's expression couldn't be more dubious. He's looking at me as if I had just told him I'd joined the Salvation Army. "Damn, I'm never driving that Chevelle again. One spin and you're talkin' contracts and owing things. And, looky there, cleaning up after yourself immediate-like. Should at least wait 'til tomorrow."

I promise Felix that I'll drop by for a beer in the next day or two and ease him out the door in a bewildered state. He follows me out to the parking lot, watches me put the blue tarp over the Chevelle, and reluctantly agrees that I can still use the car.

———

Around eight o'clock the next morning I uncover the Chevelle, stuff the tarp into the trunk, and head out Highway 26 again. I settle into the right-hand lane and give a little wave every time someone honks because they admire the vintage Chevy. I'm also having a mild argument with myself about whether chasing Richard down is the right thing to do. The house on Turner Street is a dump. Will it humiliate him if I find him living a life he would not want me to see? Is what I want to have happen worth shaming the man? But I don't turn back.

In Banks I swing by the espresso trailer again. The young woman who served me yesterday is there; she smiles with recognition—guess it makes me a regular, coming by two days in a row. I pull away, sipping my Americano, and head down Main Street with a confidence I didn't have the day before. I drive right by Turner Street, turn at the next block onto Sunset Avenue, and park in front of a house with a For Sale sign in the yard. After I finish my coffee, I step out of the car, don't see anyone concerned with my presence, and strike off. I use the only cross street to reach Turner Street and walk south toward 311 ignoring the house where Mr. Congeniality lives. I approach a decent-looking house adjacent to 311, walk onto a tidy porch filled with flower planter boxes, press the doorbell, and study the array of pansies while I wait for a response.

The woman who comes to the door is around sixty, I'd say, with graying hair and surprisingly rosy cheeks. She's short and is looking at me suspiciously through plastic-rimmed glasses. She keeps the screen door closed, so we're studying one another through a cloudy barrier of plastic mesh. She must feel safer that way.

"Yes?" she says.

I smile. "I'm inquiring about the house next door, " I say. "That one, 311." I point. "I'm looking for the man who I guess lived there until recently. His name is Richard Vickerman. Did you know him?"

She stares at me through the screen and doesn't respond. I'm about to repeat myself when she says, "And who are you?" Her voice is pleasant but wary.

"Sorry," I say. "My name is Edmund Kirby. I'm a friend of Mr. Vickerman's. I've been trying to find him." I look toward the vacant house. "Thought I'd located him, but he's gone."

She hesitates, still unsure. "You a bill collector?"

"No. Like I said, he's a friend of mine."

"He moved out near on three months ago."

"Really? Well, we haven't seen each other for many years," I explain. "I've just begun trying to reconnect with him. This is the only address I could get."

"I knew him," she says, relenting. "Didn't know him real well, but we were acquainted…in passing is all. Seemed like a nice man. Didn't seem well, though. Coughed a lot."

"Is that so? Do you happen to know where he went from here?"

"No idea. He…" She pauses and looks past me. I turn and see the owner of the green pickup hustling across the street toward us. He strides up the walk to the house.

"You okay, Miz Wilson?" He is frowning at me.

The woman pushes the screen door open and steps out onto the porch. "Now, Leroy, you just go on about your business. This gentleman and I are having a conversation."

"He was sneaking around here yesterday, and I run him off," says this Leroy. "You not get my meaning, mister? Now you better get—"

"Leroy," Mrs. Wilson raises her voice. "Did you hear me? You just go on now. This is none of your business."

"Look, fella," Leroy starts in on me. "If you—"

"Leroy!" Mrs. Wilson raises her voice another notch.

Leroy glares at me but stops his rant and backs away. When he is back across the street, Mrs. Wilson sighs and offers me a smile.

"Sorry, Mr. Kirby. Leroy can be a pain in the neck at times. He's on some sort of medication, I understand…the mental kind." She looks across the street; Leroy is standing on his porch staring at us. "Let's go inside," Mrs. Wilson says. "We can talk without being watched."

She heats some water, and we sit in her small living room sipping black tea. The house is neat, furnished with dated ranch style couch and chairs, the kind with wooden arms, knurled wooden legs, and rough-weave plaid upholstery.

"I live alone here," she says, almost as an admission of guilt. "My husband passed two years ago."

"I'm sorry to hear that," I respond.

"Bill, my husband, he used to take care of everything outside, and I kept the house," she goes on. "Now I do it all, so I'm more aware of things outdoors."

"Did you get to know Richard Vickerman at all?" I ask.

She smiles and blushes. "I have to admit that I knew him better than I said. I don't give out information about neighbors to strangers, you see."

"A good policy," I say, imagining the door knockers that assail my apartment house on a regular basis.

"Mr. Vickerman sat right where you are a few times and had a cup of tea with me." She sips from her cup. "Like I said, he wasn't well. Something with his lungs, he told me."

"You say he moved out several months ago?"

She nods. "That's right. Strange, really."

"How do you mean?" I ask.

She stares at me. "I don't know how much I should say."

I drink from my cup and don't respond. I can tell she's assessing me.

"I guess it can't hurt," she says. "You say you're a friend, isn't that so?"

"Yes, from long ago."

Mrs. Wilson sets her cup down on the lamp table beside her and folds her hands in her lap. "He lived in that poor little house for three years maybe. My husband, he used to chat with people up and down the street—he was very social. So I know he visited with Mr. Vickerman once in a while. Your friend kept to hisself, didn't come out much. Had a little blue car, but it just sat most of time. There's a little shop out the back of that place. He'd be out there a lot puttering on a rock collection, Bill said."

"You don't have any idea where he moved to?" I ask again.

She hesitates. "No, he was just gone one day...he and that woman."

"Woman? There was a woman?"

Mrs. Wilson stares at me then nods.

"Who?"

"I don't know," she answered. "Don't know who she was, where she came from, or anything."

"How long was she there…with him?"

"Not very long, maybe a month. No not even that, more like two or three weeks. Then her and Mr. Vickerman moved out. It happened quick. I never saw it, but some other folks said one morning this woman, she drove up in a rental truck, had a couple of men with her, and they emptied out the house and were gone. Less than an hour, I understand."

"What did she look like, this woman?" I ask.

Mrs. Wilson picks up her teacup, looks into it, then sets it back down. "I never got that close to her," she says. "Tall, taller than me anyhow, thin like, gray hair, shoulder-length gray hair. I started to go over there once when I saw her outside, but soon as she saw me coming she went inside quick-like. She wasn't much to look at, from what I saw, rough skin like she'd had acne as a kid, and a large nose. I remember that nose. Seemed too big for her face."

"I wish I knew where they went," I say.

"I'll ask around, Mr. Kirby," she says. "Maybe one of my neighbors heard something. If you don't mind giving me your phone number, I'll call you if I find out anything."

I scribble out my number on a slip of paper she gives me, and I hand it to her. She looks at it as if I've given her the direct line to the White House.

"Thank you, Mrs. Wilson."

"Oh sure," she says. "Your friend, Mr. Vickerman, he must be special to you, going through all this to find him."

"He is," I say. "He is. I owe him a lot. He helped set me straight many times when I was a young man, and I never ever thanked

70

him. I guess you'd call him a role model. And I…well, I just need to find him right now."

"I see," Mrs. Wilson says. She smiles and looks toward a stand of photographs arrayed on a bookcase. She points. "That picture second from the end, on the right there, that's my Aunt Mandy. She practically raised me. I was a runaway kid. Big trouble for my folks I was. Aunt Mandy, she took me in, straightened me up, and made me fly right. I owed her, too."

I'm looking at the black-and-white photograph of a woman smiling out from a silver frame. "I never got around to thanking her like I should have," says Mrs. Wilson. "I needed to tell her I was sorry for some things, too. The biggest regret of my life is that I never did. Mr. Kirby, you find your friend and do what you've set out to do."

She promises to call me if she finds out anything from her neighbors. I thank her and walk back to the car. I have a key in the door lock of the Chevelle when Leroy's Toyota pickup suddenly appears and skids up behind me. He jumps out of the truck and comes toward me. I turn to face him, electricity running up my neck, and raise a hand.

"Stop right there," I say in my best voice of warning. "You come any closer, and I will be the one calling the police."

Leroy stops in his tracks and looks a bit bewildered. "I only come to tell you something."

"That right?" I say. "What?"

"I saw 'em move the old guy out. There was three of them: a woman and two men."

"And when was this?"

"Long while back, I'd say about three or four months maybe. One morning this rent truck shows up, and two fellas do a rush job of emptying out the house of…what's the old man's name again?"

"Vickerman."

"Yeah, Vickerman. Anyway, they put all his stuff in that moving van and drove off. Then the woman, she and the old man followed the truck in that beater Honda of his. All happened real quick."

"Did you hear where they were moving?"

Leroy shakes his head. "Nah, I didn't even go over there. Like I said, didn't know the guy. Then that woman came, and she wasn't the friendly type. None of my business. But there is one thing."

"What's that?" I ask.

"That rental truck had a name on it. Would that help?"

"You mean like U-Haul?"

"No, wasn't U-Haul or anything. Was a private name." He laughs for the first time. "I had it. It was something simple like Bob's or Tom's, you know, like that. Wait, Pete's. That's it: Pete's Truck Repair and Rental, think it was."

"Pete's?" I say. "Is that a local company from here in Banks?"

"Nope. Forest Grove. Said Forest Grove on the door. Maybe your guy moved to Forest Grove," Leroy says.

"Could be," I say. "Thanks, Leroy."

Leroy grins, revealing a set of bad teeth; it may be the first time in a long time that anyone has thanked him for anything. He waves, climbs back in his little truck, toots his horn, and drives off.

Based on Leroy's tip, I drive six miles south to Forest Grove, grab a turkey and Swiss sandwich at a small café on Main Street, and ask the man who owns the place if he's heard of Pete's Truck Repair. He hasn't but offers me his Yellow Pages directory. I find the listing out on Old Highway 47 and ask for directions; Pete's is only a couple of miles from the café. Its one rental truck is parked out behind an old Quonset hut building, which is obviously serving as corporate headquarters and service center.

A vintage Kenworth dump truck is parked out in front of the garage with its hood up and two men in oily coveralls sprawled across opposing fenders their rumps up and no heads showing.

I walk over, get a visual angle on the guy closest to me, and speak up loudly. "Hi there!"

After a period of continued clanking and one curse, the man slides down. He's tall, skinny, and bald headed; he eyes me and pulls a rag from his back pocket.

"Yeah," he says and wipes at a bloodied knuckle. "What can I do for ya?"

"You rent moving trucks, I hear."

He snorts. "Got but the one truck. What ya want to move?"

"I'm not wanting to move anything, just wondering about someone who rented that truck from you awhile back, maybe three months."

He looks at me then at the Chevelle, shakes his head, and chuckles. "Dang, records that long back—good luck. I probably got 'em in there somewheres, but that truck is just a rig we have and rent once in a sunny day. You not the law, are you?"

"No," I laugh. "Just trying to locate a friend who I guess rented that truck. You Pete?"

"Ain't no Pete, least ways not since about 1964." The man looks around when another curse comes from the dump truck. "Look, I just rent that rig whenever the mood strikes me or someone really wants it and pays cash. A pain the in ass keeping it running. Figuring on getting rid of it."

"But you do have records of rentals you've made for the truck?" I ask, ending with an uptick of hope in my voice.

"Look, fella," the man wipes at his sore knuckle again, "what I got is a drawer full of receipts for cash and credit cards. Only take credit cards for my regular accounts and never for that dang truck. But if you want to paw through that stuff, yer welcome to it."

I nod, and he leads me into a sort of office full of a scattering of truck parts, empty soda pop bottles from a Coke vending machine, dust-covered automotive merchandise scattered on display shelves, and piles of paperwork on a battered desk. The guy pulls open one of the desk drawers, points into it, and walks back out to work on the dump truck.

I extricate a fistful of receipts, the kind written out on a pad with a carbon-paper copy, and begin thumbing through them. It doesn't take long to decide that I'll never figure out who bought what from Pete's, let alone who rented that truck three months ago. Except for the credit card records, almost every receipt is made out to cash for some undecipherable service. Only a few have actual names: T. Smith—fuel pump, Bob K.—brakes. I stuff the papers back into the drawer, find a worse-for-wear telephone directory, and thumb through the Vs—no Vickermans.

When I go back outside, the two mechanics are standing beside the Kenworth truck examining a hunk of metal; the bald-headed guy is turning whatever it is in his hand as if it might explain the meaning of life. The other guy, short and older, squints at me through glasses with thick lenses that are glazed with a sheen of grease. When I say thanks they just look at me.

"Nice car," the bald man says as I walk by.

I ignore him, start up the Chevelle, and goose it twice for effect before driving away from Pete's Truck Repair and Rental.

Okay Richard, where are you?

-9-

By the time I pull the Chevelle back into the apartment parking lot, I am mentally incapable of linear thought and physically spent. Other than short runs to the grocery store and back, I have not been out of this compound in months, certainly not to take on an actual objective—and certainly not to persist in achieving that objective. I pull the blue tarp out of the trunk and gently cover the car.

Felix answers my fourth knock. He looks me up and down, raises the can of beer he's holding, and waddles off to his refrigerator. I accept his offering most gratefully, pull the tab, suck off the first swallow of yeasty foam, and sigh. Felix is already on the couch, eyeballing yet another Mariner's baseball game. I settle into a much-used recliner, lean back, and begin drifting with the sounds of the ball game when Felix interrupts my slide.

"You look cooked," he's saying.

I snap awake.

"I'm thinking you didn't find him, yer guy," he says. "Am I right?"

"I'm getting closer," I say in defense.

"How close is that?"

75

I take another drink of beer. "Three months. Moved out of the place in Banks three months ago."

"But yer hot on his trail."

"I'm closer than I was sitting around here."

He turns back to the television when a roar of crowd noise comes out of the set.

"Grand slam!" he says. "Shut the door." He lifts the remote and turns off the television. "Nuther?" he asks, holding up his empty.

I shake my head. "No, I'm heading for the barn. Tired."

"Not quitting on this thing, then?" Felix says.

I yawn and raise my arms over my head. "No. Hell, Felix, I'm gaining on him." I laugh. "I can practically smell his aftershave."

He flicks the television back on, finds a *Law & Order* rerun, and settles back. I've been excused. I'm back in my apartment, thinking on what to eat, when the Princess rings. I've been expecting to hear from Andrea, but it's Mrs. Wilson from Banks.

"Yes, Mrs. Wilson," I say. "How are you?"

"Fine," she answers. "Although I've never been involved in anything like this before."

"Like what?"

"Oh, you know, snooping," she laughs. "Feel like a detective."

"I'm sorry," I say, "if this is making you uncomfortable."

"No, no, it's…well, it is kind of fun. Adds a little spice to my quiet life." Her laugh makes me smile.

"Thank you for being my detective out there," I say. "Have you had any luck?"

"Well, that's why I called, Mr. Kirby. After you left this morning, I took a walk and started calling on my neighbors, the ones nearest where Mr. Vickerman lived. I think I had five cups of tea." She laughs again. "Anyway, at first all I got was what I already know, nothing new. But then I was calling on Beulah Stewart, she's across the street from me and three houses north. Anyway, she has this little poodle dog? And she takes him for a walk 'bout four times a day."

"And did she see something?" I interrupt.

"That's what I'm coming to," she says. "Beulah, she asks me in, like I knew she would. I turned her down on the tea offer, though. I was sloshing by then." She laughs sweetly. "So, I go into my little detective story about how I was wondering whatever became of that nice old man who used to live at 311. Like that. Well now, Beulah, she up and told me just where he did go. Just spurted it out, she did."

"Really," I say. "And where is that?"

"It was like this," she goes on, "that morning, Beulah was out walking Lord Nelson, that's her dog. Silly name. Anyway, she was coming back from taking him out to do his duty, and there was that moving truck. People were hauling things out of Mr. Vickerman's house. Two men and that woman, like I told you. Beulah stopped and watched for a minute or so, and when one of the men came out carrying a box or something, she just asked where Mr. Vickerman was going." Mrs. Wilson giggles. "That's Beulah, as straightforward as they come."

"And this man told her?" I ask.

"That's right." I can hear her taking in a breath. "Mr. Kirby, your friend has moved to Vernonia."

"Vernonia?"

"That's right," she says. "Can't be but twenty-five miles or so from here."

"And this Beulah was sure that the guy said Vernonia?" I press.

"Oh yes. Beulah is a first-class gossip." She laughs. "I can guarantee she got it right. Course she didn't get to find out any more because that woman, the one I said was living with Mr. Vickerman, she came out and yelled for the man to stick to business.

Beulah said that by the time she got Lord Nelson back in the house and came out for another look, the truck was gone.

"Mr. Kirby, do you think this will help you find Mr. Vickerman?" Her voice is soft and hopeful.

"Mrs. Wilson, you are wonderful!"

She giggles. "I hope so. It was fun, really. I've never done anything like this before. But you go find your friend now and…and tell him how important he was to you."

"I will," I respond. "I surely will."

"I only wish I'd done that with my aunt Mandy."

I promise to let her know how things turn out, and we disconnect.

Andrea isn't home when I call; so I leave a voice mail, make a peanut butter and banana sandwich, go to bed early, and stare at the ceiling. Vernonia is keeping me awake.

———

It's only Wednesday, but it seems like this all began weeks ago. I've been up since six, didn't sleep, and already driving to Vernonia after a bowl of Cheerios and a cup of coffee. The Chevelle is running smoothly. It is a bright spring day. Trees are flowering all over the place; new leaves are bright on the tress—Sylvia liked all this "signs of spring" stuff. All I knew about spring was that the grass grew three times as fast and I had to mow the lawn three times as often.

I pass through the little burg of Manning, known for its only national-brand business, a Dairy Queen, and a few miles farther on swing off Highway 26. Vernonia is fifteen miles away. I throttle back, try to enjoy the scenery, but my nerves are on full alert. Is Richard really out here? If this had gone as written in my head, I'd have driven out to Banks, knocked on the door at 311 Turner Street, and Richard would have answered. We would hug and have this remember-the-old-days talk I've been imagining. But how would Richard, the Dick Vic I knew, how would he respond to my sense of obligation to him, to my intended expressions of debt and my need to have him hear me out as he once did?

I feel impatience rise again and press on the accelerator. The Chevelle surges forward, and I roar beneath three old railroad trestles, the last one a huge maze of crisscrossing timbers and support poles rising high above the roadway. Suddenly Vernonia appears; I stab the brakes, slow abruptly, and ease into a right-hand turn onto Bridge Street, which turns out to be the main street through town. I pass a very new-looking city hall, an assortment of operable businesses (hardware store, bank, restaurants, coffee roaster) mixed in with a smattering of empty storefronts—every business fighting for its share of a smaller pie. The Chevelle lopes down the street and crosses a low-rise concrete bridge; the sign says Rock Creek. I pass the high school, a flat-roofed brick building of a style common in the fifties. Right next to it is the elementary school, a much older structure, maybe built in the thirties or forties.

Okay, nice little town, but how the hell do I find Richard? I turn around at the fire station and double back to the city hall, where a woman at the counter tells me that unless someone has a utility bill, a listed phone number, or is in some other way known in the area, there's no way she can help me. She runs a check of local water and sewer users and phone listings. No Vickermans. I'm not surprised.

I gas up at the Shell station and ask the owner, a lanky fellow with a great smile, if he's had an older blue Honda gas up there.

"Old blue Honda," he says. "Accord or Civic?"

"That I don't know," I answer. "Just blue, light blue maybe."

"Yeah I see 'em, Honda's like that, but got no names for you."

"I'm trying to find a friend who I've been told moved out here and drives a car like that. If I leave my phone number, would you call if one comes in for gas? I'm looking for an older man, in his seventies, and a woman, gray hair, but younger than the man."

I scribble my number on my gas receipt and hand it to the man. He squints at me but takes it. "Don't worry," I say, "just a friend I haven't seen in years, and I'm trying to locate him. Okay?"

The man nods.

"Thanks, Mister..."

"Huff," he answers, "Chuck Huff."

"Thanks, Chuck."

"Can't promise anything, I'm not here all the time."

"I understand," I say.

He sticks my phone number in his shirt pocket. "I'll tell the other guys to keep an eye out."

I'm giving the Chevelle's big engine a workout driving the neighborhoods. It's a small town, but I still have to go up and down all the streets looking in driveways, behind buildings, stopping and staring, peering. I receive more than one hard stare along with the usual smiles for the Chevelle. I see a little blue car on E Street and get out to take a closer look, but it's a Toyota. After an hour of circling the streets of Vernonia, I visit a pub on Bridge Street and have an ale with a pastrami sandwich, using up almost all the cash I have with me. I ask the young woman behind the counter if she's seen a man of Richard's description, as close as I know it anyway, or a blue Honda. She smiles, revealing great teeth, and says no.

After lunch I get smart late and go back to the city hall to pick up a map of the town; the same woman is there and is happy to oblige. I can sort of figure out what parts of town I've already covered and circle them with a pencil, fully realizing that the car could have been gone when I drove a street and is now back. I concentrate on another section I guess west of City Hall and drive the streets until I decide I might attract the wrong kind of attention if I continue my detecting. I head for home.

I'm back in the apartment parking lot by four o'clock. I put the tarp back over the car, go to the bank of mailboxes, and put my key in mine for the first time in a couple of weeks. A wad of junk mail is wedged in so tightly I have to rip it out one piece at a time. Other than the electric and telephone bills, plus a notice from the apartment manager that I'm overdue with my rent check, everything else can be recycled; I take a side trip to the Dumpster and recycle the old-fashioned way.

My fatigue is a surprise; you'd think I just spent a day unloading freight at Singleton's. I take the last beer in the fridge over to the couch, sit, kick off my shoes, and study the Vernonia town map. Town isn't that big. Should be able to find one blue Honda. I can't imagine who the woman is, why she just evidently showed up and moved in with Richard, and—even stranger—why the sudden exodus?

The Princess jingles; I push up off the couch and grab it before it can ring a third time.

"Edmund!" It's Andrea. "I've been calling and calling—you just have to get an answering machine. Where have you been?"

"Hi," I say.

She takes a breath and calms down. "I'm sorry. It's just that… where have you been, and what have you found out? I got the message about Daddy maybe being in Vernonia. I hardly ever check that answering machine, Edmund. I saw the light blinking this morning, but you were already gone, I guess. Everyone calls me on my cell."

"Sorry," I say.

"Yeah…well, we have to get you to use twenty-first century telecommunications. How can you stand not being in touch?"

"I get along," I say smiling.

"Barely, I'd say." She inhales. "So, about my dad, do you really think he's in Vernonia now?"

"As far as I know, yes. But I'm only going on tips from the neighbors in Banks."

Her breathing is more even. "This is getting weirder and weirder. What next? Are you going out there? To Vernonia?"

"I've been there," I say. "Just got back."

"Did you find him?" she asks. "No, you didn't find him."

"You're right, I didn't find him," I say, "or the woman."

"Woman? What woman?" Her voice rises. "Edmund, what are you talking about? You haven't said anything about a woman."

"I was getting around to it," I say. "Wanted to ease into it."

"You mean a woman like living with my father?"

"Seems so."

Andrea is quiet for a moment. "Why, that old bastard," she says finally.

"Living with another woman. Did you see her?"

"Andrea, I haven't even found them yet," I say. "I only have a general description of her."

"Bet she's some young bimbo," she says, snapping her words out.

I laugh. "Will you listen to yourself? Your dad is an old man, and he may be ill. Besides, the woman doesn't sound like any spring chicken or raving beauty."

"Ill? What do you mean?"

"A woman, a neighbor in Banks said she thought he had some lung problems. Sorry, forgot to mention that."

"You're forgetting to mention a number of things." She sighs. "What now?"

"Well, I have some feelers out in Vernonia," I say, keeping to myself that my one feeler is the gas station owner. "I'll go back out tomorrow."

"What will you do?"

"Oh, drive the streets looking for the blue Honda your dad's supposed to own. And I ask people if they've seen anyone meeting his or the woman's description. He's not listed in the phone book or anywhere else I can find."

"This is all so weird," she says.

"Did you close your real estate deals?" I ask.

"One. Still have two to go before Friday."

"I thought maybe you'd like to go with me to Vernonia. Look around."

"No," she says, her voice a whisper. "I thought I could, but… maybe when you find him, then I'll go."

"If I find him."

"Yes, if you find him."

I promise to keep her informed. She gives me her cell phone number.

"I'll find him," I say.

-10-

"Good morning, Mr. Kirby," says Mrs. Wilson. "I hope I'm not calling too early."

I assure her that she isn't as I hold the Princess with my shoulder and finish frying two eggs and a piece of bologna—my power breakfast.

"Well, I promised to let you know if I heard anything more about your friend," she goes on. "Mr. Vickerman. Have you found him yet?"

"No, not yet. And did you learn something more?" I prompt.

"Oh…well, you see, Lucille Peters, she lives two houses down on the other side of the 311 house from me. Anyway, she got wind of how I've been asking around for you about Mr. Vickerman." She laughs. "I'm getting a reputation."

"Better watch out."

She laughs some more.

"So what about Mrs. Peters?"

"Okay, Lucille told me that she'd once passed a word with the woman who was in the house before Mr. Vickerman moved away. I expect she's the only one that ever got a word out of that woman. She wasn't friendly in the least."

"What did this Lucille find out?"

"It's not much, really, but I thought you'd want to know. She said she was Mr. Vickerman's sister. The woman did. Think maybe that's a way to connect with your friend?"

"Maybe," I say and thank her for calling.

I'm in Vernonia by nine o'clock, ready to cover the town street by street. I have a new sense of urgency because of Mrs. Wilson's phone call. Richard has a younger brother. He has no sister.

As soon as I pull into the Shell station, Chuck Huff spots me and comes over. "Glad to see you," he says. "Tried to call but didn't get an answer. Think I have an address for you." He pulls a slip of paper out of his shirt pocket. "Blue Honda came in yesterday not long after you were here. A woman was driving. She seemed to look sort of like you described. Here's the address. Got it off her check."

He hands me the piece of paper and looks around. "This is on the q.t. I'm not in the habit of giving out customers' private info as a regular practice."

"I understand," I say. "Don't worry. I'm looking for a friend. I'm not a bounty hunter."

"Glad to hear it," he says.

"Now where's Mississippi Avenue?" I ask.

I follow his directions, pass the high school, and make a left turn onto Texas Avenue, a street that rises slowly in a gentle arc. The Chevelle climbs the short hill easily. I find Mississippi Avenue and drive down its gravelly surface, searching for a house numbered 503. When I spot it, I drive on until the street ends on Louisiana, turn around in the last driveway, and come back, stopping two houses back. A blue Honda is there, parked in the short gravel drive next to an old orange Ford Pinto station wagon. The house is a squat bungalow with its wooden siding painted a chalky looking pale green. The yard is a rough-cut weedy patch of grass with a Port Orford cedar struggling to decorate one corner of the house. A Dish TV antenna is attached to the roof. I turn off the ignition, the Chevelle rumbles dead, and I sit back and watch for signs of life.

85

Nothing, no activity, and it's been nearly ten minutes. I get out of the car, look around, hitch up on my pants, and saunter up the street, gravel popping and crunching beneath my feet. I stand on the street, my stomach churning, and study the house. Dismal thing. Blinds are pulled down. Dick Vic is in there; at least I think he is. A man well into his seventies by now, and I'm coming up on my fiftieth.

God, I was two weeks shy of twenty when I first went to work for Bob-Buys, working my way through college until I knocked up Sylvia. Back in those days, grocery stores dealt with rack-jobbers who ordered and stocked all the sundries, everything from aspirin to nylons. That's what the Bob-Buys Company did, and Richard Vickerman was warehouse manager when I first started. He trained me to be a picker, the person who pulled the orders and packed them. Then the orders would be shipped to some drop points where guys wearing ties would run around in Ford Econoline vans and stock the shelves. Dick Vic covered my ass a lot my first months on the job. For some reason I kept mixing up the pick numbers for certain items, like packing a case of Super Tampax instead of Peterson's Peanut Brittle. Easy to do: transpose a 008 code for an 800 code.

I wonder what Richard looks like now? Will he recognize me; even know me? I'm standing in the street at the head of the driveway, staring at the house, when a woman suddenly comes out on the small porch. She is slender, has shoulder-length gray hair, and is wearing blue jeans and a red and blue plaid man's shirt. She stands with hands in her pockets.

"What do you want?" she says loudly in a voice that brooks no hospitality.

I force up a smile, give a wave, and start down the short drive.

"We don't want nothing." She's saying.

"I'm not selling anything," I say in a raised voice.

"Who are you then? That your car?" She turns her head and I nod. "Why you standing out here looking?"

She watches as I approach. Her face is lean and pocked with acne scars; her nose is painfully globular. "What do you want?" she repeats.

"My name's Edmund Kirby," I say. "I'm looking for Richard Vickerman."

She reaches up and runs fingers through her hair and doesn't take her eyes off me. "No one by that name here. Never heard of no Vickerman." She speaks too quickly, kicks it out like a recorded message.

"What about 311 Turner Street in Banks?" I bluff.

She blinks. "That supposed to mean something?" she says.

"You lived at that address maybe three months ago, you and Richard."

"That right? What makes you think that?"

"People on Turner Street, they remember Richard and you."

"Well, they're crazy," she says and pulls a pack of cigarettes out of her shirt pocket.

"Didn't you rent a truck from Pete's Truck Repair in Forest Grove about three months ago?"

She doesn't answer, just stares at me.

"Seems that that's when Richard Vickerman moved from Tuner Street," I say. "In Banks." I wait a couple of breaths and ask, "That ring any bells with you?"

She pulls out a Bic lighter and ignites her cigarette. She draws on it. "So who is this person to you?" she asks. "Vickerman, you say?"

"He and I go back a long way," I say, "nearly thirty years. I lost track of him."

She studies me but doesn't voice another denial. We stare at one another. A UPS truck rumbles by.

"I'm not here to bother him," I say. "I just want to say hello, you know, reconnect. That's all. We were close once."

She exhales a stream of smoke, turns like she's going to go inside, but stops. I know Richard is in there for sure.

"Can I see him? We really are friends."

"Don't matter," she says with the aplomb of a seasoned gate-keeper. "He don't see folks anymore."

"How come?"

She chews on her lip and doesn't blink. Doesn't answer, either. "Are you his sister?"

Her eyes widen. "What makes you say that?"

"Isn't that what you told people in Banks?"

"Nosey busybodies," she says. "Told 'em that to stop their darn questions."

"You married to him, then?" I probe.

The short pivot of her head is a no, and what else? That she wouldn't ever want that? Or she wants what cannot be? "What is your name again?" she asks. I tell her; and she points at the ground like she's pegging me down, tells me to wait here, and goes back into the house.

She comes back out in a few minutes and stands on the small front porch looking down at me. She folds her arms across her chest like a man would.

I raise my eyebrows; she shakes her head. "He can't be moved," she says. "Like I said."

"Did you tell him who it is?"

"Yep. Makes no never mind. Don't feel bad. There's been others. He sent 'em away, too. No one comes anymore."

"Really?" I say. "You told him who I was—Edmund Kirby. You told him."

"Look, mister, I told him. You hearing me?" Her face is even more unfriendly. So here we stand at the boundary of Dick Vic's isolation.

"And you?" I say with added cheer. "Are you not accepting visitors?"

It's like watching an Etch A Sketch: her annoyance is wiped away and she laughs. "Me?"

"The thing is…what's your name, ma'am?"

She blows air out through closed lips. "Ma'am," she says, like I'd just farted. "I'm Twyla."

"Twyla. Okay. Thing is, Twyla, I'm in a state of urgency here. May I use your bathroom?"

She studies me, suspicion filling her eyes. "He's not gonna see you, fella."

"I understand," I say. "I just really need to use your bathroom."

She raises her arm and makes a reluctant motion for me to follow her. I brace myself for imagined strange odors, expecting a dark, closed-up hole of a place. There is a closed-in airlessness and the scent of something cooked earlier. The furniture in the small living room is dated and worn, but the place is neat. A big-screen television dominates one corner, along with a bookshelf that is filled top to bottom with videos. Twyla points the way to the bathroom. I lean over the commode with relief and stare down at the stack of magazines on the toilet water tank. The one on top is *Lapidary Journal.* I finish, zip up; flush and, while the water is circling, I thumb through *Gem World*, a magazine on rock hounding, cutting, polishing. Looks like Mrs. Wilson was right about Richard working on rocks. It's odd to come back into someone's life after years of separation and try to make sense of his habits and his habitat, let alone presenting him with who you've become.

Twyla's waiting for me; she plants her feet and halts the platform rocker she's sitting in. "Have a seat…if you want," she says.

I sit on the arm of a threadbare couch and look around. "So, where's the man of the house?"

She hesitates. "His shop. Back bedroom's been turned into his shop. Rocks," she says, "thunder eggs, actually. Nothing but thunder eggs. Works on them rocks all the time. Cuts 'em open, polishes 'em." She points and, sure enough, every table and shelf has thunder eggs on it. "He cuts 'em and—bingo—there's agate, jasper, opal, and the like inside."

"Oregon's state rock," I say.

She curls her mouth like she's saying: *Tell me something new.*

"This is a pretty one." I hold up a rock half the size of a knobby dumpling with a polished amber agate center.

"Oh, they're pretty all right. Give 'em that."

"I don't get it. Why won't he see me? Something I'm missing here?"

She sobers and looks over and past me. "We live quiet. Keep to ourselves." She lowers her eyes then looks back into mine. "We like it that way, frankly."

"We?" I ask.

"Look, I don't want to be rude here, but the man says he doesn't want to see you. It's that simple, nothing else."

"What would happen if I just went back there? Right now, walked in?" I raise my eyebrows.

Twyla draws her lips in and pouts her answer. "Door's bolted."

We sit quietly for a few minutes; she rocks gently and examines her nails, and I look the room over, count thunder eggs. About twenty scattered about, I think. Of course, I'm wondering about this woman and Dick Vic and what they are to one another. Strange the way people can pair up and how they are together, often enduring bizarre behavior in their mates. Where did Twyla find Richard, and what keeps them together? I'm thinking that Twyla's around sixty, maybe late fifties. And I know Richard has her beat by fifteen years or more. That makes the connection factor even more interesting.

"So, Twyla," I say, my rock inventory over, "how long have you known Dick Vic—I mean Richard? Always called him Dick Vic. Everybody did. What do you call him?"

"Richard," she says. "Just call him Richard. Known him for a while."

I bob my head and wait to see if she will go farther than that. "A while? How long is that?"

"Coffee, bacon, eggs and cakes," she says, ignoring my question. "That's how I met him. Charlene's Café in Banks. I have a little housecleaning business. A couple of my customers are in Banks, so I catch breakfast at Charlene's ever so often. One day Richard, he brought one of these eggs with him into Charlene's, set it out on the counter, didn't say a word. Charlene saw that dang rock and went all gooey over it. Came down the counter to me holding the thing: *Ain't this the purtyist rock.* I was rolling it in my hand, admiring it, when the guy said: *Thunder egg. That's what they're called. Thunder eggs.* That's how we met. Nothing fancy."

"Never underestimate a man and his rocks," I say.

She blinks and looks bored at my naughty humor.

"So lightening struck at the café, and you moved in with him?"

She squints. "That any of your business?"

I smile and shrug. "Curious."

She inhales hard, lights up another cigarette, and stares at me. "Okay, yeah moved in with Richard at his place in Banks. Probably your snoops there told you I lived there for a month or so. Then we decided to move in together. This place is cheaper, so he moved in with me lock, stock, and rocks. My husband was killed in the woods a long time back. This place and the mortgage is all he left behind. I lived alone a long time."

"So you saw one thunder egg and decided to move in with the guy?"

She hesitates. "Let's say we formed a merger. Keeps the wolf at

91

bay, anyway." She leans back and folds her arms. "So now, that enough to satisfy you?"

"Should it be?"

"Better be. Like I said, he don't want to see you. No sense in pushing it."

"Well, I'll tell you, Twyla: I'm not quitting on this, not yet. Not until I see the eyeballs of the man I knew. I think I'll just come back, say in a week. Wait him out. What do you think?"

"Don't listen, do you?" Her voice gets edgy.

"Look," I say, "the man was as close to me as you can get without blood. I'm coming back. What are you going to do, call the cops?"

"Could. Might, too."

"I don't think so." We stare at each other.

"Hell then, knock yourself out. Has to be Tuesday, though, when I'm around. I don't have any houses to clean on Tuesdays. That's the deal. Take it our leave it. Or I will call the police."

"Tuesdays?"

She bobs her head. "That's right. Don't mean he'll see you, but still don't want you harassing him. He's sick."

"That so?"

"Lungs. Bad lungs."

Tuesday it is. Twyla hands me the paper and pencil I ask for and watches, frowning, while I write a note to Richard. She consents to give it to him. *Hey Dick Vic, Tell me again, does the code for Super Tampax start with 800 or 008? I'll get the answer next week. Edmund.*

Twyla stands on the porch as I walk back to the Chevelle. I swear I can feel the heat from her eyes make a warm spot between my shoulder blades. I drive past the house slowly and give a wave; Twyla is just staring, no response. Something cold rolls over in my stomach.

-11-

Around six the phone rings. It's Andrea. In a soft voice she asks, "Did you find him?" She is hesitant, almost as if she is wincing, not really sure she wants me to answer.

"Yeah. I did."

"Really?" Her voice is breathy.

"This is all so bizarre. Really strange. How is he?"

"I didn't get to see him. He wouldn't see me. Won't see anyone, I guess. He's living with a woman—remember I told you that? Anyway, she's his enforcer, his gatekeeper."

"I'm having a hard time with that. My father living with another woman." The rate of her breathing picks up, and her voice deepens. "I knew I shouldn't do this. Who is she, this woman? Is she younger? I'll bet she is."

I laugh. "Come on, Andrea, what's it matter? But, yeah, she's younger, but still around sixty, I think. Don't worry: no children in the offing, I figure."

"Very funny."

"According to her, they're living together to make ends meet. Her name's Twyla, by the way. Guess your dad spends all his time cutting and polishing thunder eggs. This Twyla, she cleans houses to bring in extra money—so she says"

"Thunder eggs? You mean those lumpy rocks?"

"Yeah, cutting and polishing rocks. That's how he spends his time."

"My dad a rock hound? I don't believe it."

"Saw a bunch of rocks, all cut and polished."

"Yeah, well, whatever. But you saw where he's living?"

"Yeah, I was in the house…briefly."

"But you didn't actually see him," she says. "How do you know it's really him living with this woman?"

"I don't. I'm just assuming. But the woman fits the description given me by the people in Banks. He's there, all right, and I'm going back Tuesday to try to see him again. This Twyla doesn't clean houses on Tuesdays. So that's the only day of the week she'll let me come. Says she's protecting him from harassment. And she reminded me that he doesn't want to see me, anyway."

"That is strange."

"I know. The Dick Vic I knew would want to see me. But people change."

"All right, say he is a recluse. What next?" she asks.

"If I see him, rather, if he'll see me, we'll talk. That's all I want to do. If he won't next Tuesday, I'll go again."

The sound of her deep breath surges in my ear. "And all this is so you can decide the direction of your life by talking with my father who's hiding out, polishing rocks, and shacked up with a woman named Twyla?"

"Andrea, I have to do this."

"I know," she says. "I'm sorry. Please, can I see you next Tuesday? I want to know how he is, too. Can we meet for dinner or something? Or you could come here. I'll cook."

"Okay, sure," I say. "I might not know anything. Of course, you can go with me next Tuesday to see for yourself."

Her laugh is hesitant. "Not yet."

"Why not?"

"I don't know, just…" she quits talking.

"What?" I ask.

"It scares me," she says, "maybe seeing my father living a bizarre, crazy life."

"Okay, we'll take a step at a time."

———————

I have to say, the time I've spent waiting until this Tuesday morning has been a test. Every bit of me has wanted to climb into the Chevelle, roar back out to Vernonia, rush into the house where Richard is, and roust him out. I mean, I couldn't sleep in, couldn't even enjoy spending half the day in bed like I'd become accustomed to. The one measurable bit of action I took was accosting Felix out on the grounds to ask him if I could keep using the car. He gave me this long look, shook his head at my focused energy, blew smoke in my face, and said yes. I'm a big disappointment to him, I know.

There's a greater exhilaration in rousing the Chevelle this morning, bringing 350 horses to life and giving the car its head out on the freeway, ducking into the Vista Ridge Tunnel and heading west out 26. I smile a bit, passing through the tunnel and hearing the throaty rumble from the car magnified.

Twyla is on the front porch, sitting on a kitchen chair, when I park the Chevelle behind the blue Honda. She is smoking a cigarette and has one leg up on a wooden box. She flicks the butt out into the yard and stands up.

"Didn't think you'd come back," she says.

I shrug. "I know you didn't. I came anyway."

"Waste of your time."

"Maybe. He here?"

She nods.

"Does he know I'm coming?"

She nods again.

"Change his mind?"

"Nope. Like I said, he don't want to see you."

"Is he hiding out with his eggs?" I ask.

"Only room that has a lock. Otherwise you could run him to ground. He has no choice but to bolt the door."

We go into the house. I make a pointing motion down the hall. She shrugs her permission, and I tiptoe up to the door and put an ear against it. I hear some shuffling around. I raise a fist but hesitate and look back at Twyla; she is chewing on her lip, frowning. My first blow is more of a tap. I say his name. Nothing. I hit the door harder; it rattles a bit on its hinges. There is no response and no more sounds, but a sudden coughing jag begins as I'm turning away. These are chest-deep coughs; they go on in peals of four or five in a row then start again. I lower my head and listen up next to the door and feel the dread of knowing something isn't right.

Twyla is standing where I left her staring at me, her face void of expression, her eyes staring into me. I raise my arms, questioning, and she signals for me to follow and goes back out onto the porch. She has her hands in the back pockets of her jeans and is looking off across the graveled street.

"That sounds terrible," I say. "I know he's sick, but just how sick is he?"

"Bad, real bad," she says. "Doctors call it COPD, chronic obstructive pulmonary disease."

"Emphysema?"

"Yeah, goes with it. He just says he's a lunger now. Been getting worse."

"Still smoking?" I ask, remembering Richard with a Chesterfield cigarette burning most all the time, between his fingers, between his lips, or smoldering in an ashtray. He switched to menthols when someone told him they were better for the lungs. Great theory.

"Nope. Hasn't smoked since I've known him," she says.

"All this rock grinding business can't be helping his lungs any,"

I say. "Pretty dusty. isn't it?"

"What the hell difference does it make now? Rocks are what's keeping him alive, I think. Without them, who knows? Probably die from nothing to do."

"Is there a way in around back of the house?" I ask, turning to step off the porch.

"That's locked, too," she says.

Our eyes meet. "I'm going to break in," I say.

Twyla shakes her head slowly and squints at me. "No, yer not doing any such a thing."

I'm considering my options. I can feel Twyla taking the measure of what I might be thinking of doing.

"Tell you this, fella: you make a move to knocking doors in and I'll call the cops quicker'n you can imagine."

"Maybe I'll just have to do it anyway," I say.

Twyla steps down off the porch, walks out a few feet, and lights up another cigarette. Her back is to me; I can't decide if I'm being shunned or if she is considering what to do about me. A car passes on the street. She turns around to face me and walks back.

"I'm supposed to tell you that he doesn't want you to come back," she says. "That he has nothing to say to you."

"You just make that up? Doesn't sound like Dick Vic to me."

She tosses the half-smoked cigarette on the ground and stomps on it. "You know, yer getting under my skin. What do you need, a truckload of lumber to fall on yer head before you get the message? He don't want to see you. I don't want you comin' around. Now get in yer...yer hot car out there and don't come back."

I smile. "Bravo! You're one tough lady. You his secretary of defense, is that it?"

We stare at each other; she's a stone face, and I'm smiling.

"I'm not giving up, Twyla," I say. I raise a hand. "I'm not going to push it any more today, but...I'm not sure how you two

97

fit together, that for sure is none of my business. At least, I don't think so."

"It ain't."

"The thing is," I say, hooking a thumb over my shoulder toward the house, "that man and I were close. So I'll be back."

"Waste of time. Old coot won't never give in, I tell you, he won't."

"Maybe." I look straight at her. "Anyway, think I'll give it another go or two."

She stares back for a moment. Her face goes hard, but then she shrugs and toes the gravel. "No skin off'n me. Has to be Tuesdays, though. Sick as he is, I gotta be around in case he gets agitated."

-12-

Twyla's watching me write Richard another note; this time I slide it under the door to his shop and yell out that I'll be seeing him again. *Richard, Remember when I mixed up orders to six different customers? What a mess. They wanted my head, but you stood by me and told me it wasn't the end of the world. You told me we'd get through the adversity. Just keep smiling, you said. Our mantra became "Smile in the face of adversity" and it got us through many tough moments. Richard, I need to connect with that person again, just for a moment. I'll be back. Edmund.*

––––––––––

Just outside Manning, the Chevelle begins to buck and snort. I limp into the gravel parking lot of an empty storefront and have my head under the hood when a kid tonguing an ice cream cone wanders up. He stands, licking a glob of something green, watching me stick my hand into places too hot to touch like I actually know what I'm doing. I feel his eyes on me, and I keep probing as if the laying on of hands would heal the machine. I'm sucking on seared fingertips when, in a flat voice, the kid says, "Jerry can fix that." He points his dripping cone in a straight line across the highway and, sure enough, there is Jerry's Auto doing business out of an old gas station. I manage to cajole Jerry out from under a pickup and, with a show of anguish I suggest he may be the man to get the Chevy running on all eight again. A skinny guy, young but balding, beak nose, wearing coveralls with a rip at one knee, stands, wiping his hands on a grease rag.

He glances across at the car, worries the rag some more. "Okay, drive it over here and park it under the canopy there, and I'll take a look."

I get the Chevelle running, goose it enough to sputter across the highway, and park where I was told. The guy has gone back to tinker with the pickup, so I stand by patiently so as not to spook him into saying he hasn't got time. When at last he wanders back out, his eyes widen.

"Holy cow," he says, "a Super Sport Chevelle. What year?"

"Nineteen seventy," I answer.

"What's in there, 454 or 396 cubic inches?"

I calmly say, "396, 350 horse, turbo 400 tranny."

He pulls the pins, pops the hood, and looks in. "Damn, I always wanted one of these. It's running rough? Man, would ya look at that. Old muscle."

"Yeah," I say, "it hasn't been getting much use. Sits a lot. I expect it needs some attention."

He is bracing himself on the left fender, leaning over, bobbing and weaving, craning his neck. "If it's been sittin', could be bad wire, dead plug, or maybe the Quadra Jet's gummed up. Could be the automatic choke's stuck open, too."

"Uh-huh." I hum like *sure-you-betcha what I figured too.*

Jerry is smiling. "Never had my hands on one of these. Tell you what, got about five minutes left buttoning up that pickup there before I can get to this. Then I'll check it out. That okay?"

"I'm not going anywhere." I swivel my head around. "Maybe I'll walk up and get me a cone." I wink at the kid who followed me over and has by now finished his cone; all that remains is a green halo around his mouth. The boy responds not at all to my chummy wink, and Jerry the mechanic is emoting over cubic inches. I have been dismissed. I cross the highway and walk up to the Dairy Queen.

I opt for the straight vanilla soft cone with the curly Q, the kind I remember as a kid, and saunter back on the highway shoulder, dust blowing up in my eyes every time a semi throttles by. The vanilla is licked down flat, and I'm beginning to nibble on the cone when I first see the place: a small wooden building set back from the road, fronted by a potholed, sparsely graveled parking lot.

The building is nearly invisible behind a wall of hanging baskets and a porch awash in young shrubs in plastic buckets, a stack of planter boxes, and trays of petunias and pansies, begonias—spring is here. I make out the words on a weathered wooden sign to be *Wood Glen Nursery*. I look up the road and can make out the mechanic's rear end protruding from beneath the hood of the Chevelle. He is still deciphering the beast's upset. What the hell, I might find a plant I like and let it die of neglect just for spite. It could be a test of how far I've slipped back into normality.

The store is a jumble of plant stuff and odors. Boxes of bone meal, plant food, and slug bait combine to give the place a nose-teasing musty smell. A Help Wanted sign is taped to the wall behind the sales counter, but there is not a soul in the place. I keep licking and nibbling and detour out through an open back door onto a dock cluttered with an assortment of gardening tools and bags of mulch and clay pots. Beyond that, there opens up an imposing yard of nursery stock: shrubs, trees, flowers—I mean, the place is a rain forest, a botanical garden. And from out of a stand of potted saplings emerges a woman wearing a broad-brimmed straw hat, white tee shirt, and denim bib overalls, carrying a plastic planter tub with a small young tree in it. She sets it down when she sees me, sets her jaw, and strides over. Her eyes are like hot, black rivets, and her skin is taut and coppery, her arms slender but muscled. She looks up at me from ground level and pulls off leather gloves.

"Something I can do for you?" she says, thwacking the gloves in her hand.

I swallow the big gob of sugar cone and melting goo and have to cough to clear my throat. The woman watches me with no change in expression. "Sorry," I say, my eyes watering, "just looking around."

She looks away and her attentiveness shifts, as is the tendency of people with things to do and the mental edge to be annoyed when distracted.

"Fella up the road, mechanic, is working on my car…I just wandered over," I explain. "Nice place."

The woman harrumphs, jams the gloves in a back pocket, and brushes her hands together before bringing them to rest on her hips. "If it don't kill me," she says. "You wouldn't be looking for work, would you now?" She squints at me. "Been trying to do it all myself but this time of year it's a bear."

"I'll bet," I say, licking the ends of my fingers and wiping them on the butt of my pants. "Saw your Help Wanted sign, but I'm not much of a green thumb, I'm afraid."

She puts a thumb up against her nose and clears a nostril. "Not lookin' for a damn botanist. Need someone who can point a hose, make change, and lift at least fifty pounds. Hell, I can lift a hundred." She takes off her straw hat and wipes her forehead with the back of a hand, puts it back on, and shakes her head. "I'm not thinking straight," she says. "You look like a fella works inside, probably runs a computer."

"I don't know," I hear myself speaking, can't stop. "Might give me a good change of pace."

Her name is Glenda Wood. I get it: Glenda Wood, Wood Glen Nursery. Fact is, she goes by Glen. She walks me through the nursery stock, and I agree that I can drag a hose around, repot stock with proper instructions, lift bags of mulch, and make change. I would say she is about forty, a hard forty—probably wears leather underwear and sleeps on a moss mattress.

I walk back up the highway to Jerry's Auto, questioning my sanity. Jerry has the Chevelle purring; he replaced a bad spark plug wire. He tries to seduce me into bringing the car back in for a full tune-up. I give him a maybe, and he accepts the sixteen bucks I have in my wallet as payment. I thank him and drive the short distance to Wood Glen, go in, and water plants for half an hour or so then tell Glen I'll see her tomorrow or sometime. She is okay with me picking my own hours, and we agree on maybe twenty hours a week—around that. We leave it loose.

I round out an eventful day by showing up at Andrea's, well scrubbed and carrying a bottle of red wine I took a chance on because it had an artsy label and was cheap. She greets me at the door, breathy, smelling fresh and lemony, and too enthusiastic about the wine. I've taken some care in cleaning myself up and picking the best clothes I own: charcoal slacks, light yellow dress shirt, and my trusty loafers.

Andrea looks nice; I mean very appealing in a high-collared white blouse and blue slacks. A thin gold necklace graces her neck, and those blue eyes of hers are wide and hopeful, I think, or rather I assume. The house is an enormous English Tudor, hers, I learn, by right of property settlement. Her object lesson is that if you choose a mate poorly, at least marry significant assets. I bet Sylvia's been thinking the same thing, regretfully so.

We're dining on clams tossed in pasta with a light cream sauce, steamed green beans—the very thin ones—and a baguette of French bread; it's a step up from frozen macaroni and cheese. So my red wine fits right in and has shoulders after all and wins an appreciative nod from Andrea.

"So, tell me about where he lives," Andrea says.

I stall, turn a roll of pasta onto my fork, and wonder how best to describe her father's living conditions.

"It's just that…he's, you know, on my mind so much now," she continues. "Since you first called I've been thinking of him—a lot. Wondering what he must look like now and how he lives. Is this place where he lives a hovel? Is he well? What has he been doing all this time?" She sighs and puts her fork down. "It's always there, you know. You go on with your life, make your way…and your mistakes. But back here," she touches the back of her head with a finger tip, "right here, is where my derelictions have set up housekeeping. My father comes to me there when I'm least expecting him, with the same question: *Have you forgotten me?*" She grasps her wineglass and gulps from it and puts a hand over her mouth, but she can't restrain the tears.

"No, he's not well. He's sick, I guess real sick," I say. Get that part over with. "Chronic lung disease. Isn't smoking now, but all those years of sucking on Chesterfields have caught up with him. Like I said, I didn't see him first hand, heard him coughing is all. This woman, Twyla, she says it's not good." Andrea stares at me without blinking but says nothing. I go on. "Okay, where he lives. The house is a tired bungalow type, I guess you'd call it. The two of them manage life in their own way, you know pooling what they have."

"Are they…do they love one another?" she asks. "You think?"

"Who can tell about that?" I say. "Until the day I found out my wife was leaving me, I would've told anyone asking that, yeah, we loved one another. Your dad? I have no idea. My gut feeling is that, you know, that maybe they just look out for each other. Beyond that, I haven't a clue."

There is nothing more to say, really—how can anyone judge whether two people are devoted or merely tolerant of one another? I've been there, and I got it right, didn't I? Andrea seems content with what I tell her, or at least accepting. After twisting our words over and around what is and what is not, we adjourn from the dining room to the kitchen. She makes coffee, and we enjoy some cheesecake with it and avoid any more talk of Richard. We clear the table just a bit—this isn't about domesticity—go into the living room and settle onto a long leather couch. A floral fragrance rises from a bowl of dried flower petal potpourri sitting on the coffee table. Andrea pours us each a snifter of brandy; it's all so civilized. I watch her and try to remember the stunning young girl I was attracted to thirty years ago. But all I see is a mature woman, a person with mileage on her, just like all of us now, with lines of richness and lines of loss around her eyes and her mouth.

She sits beside me; we touch our glasses and hesitantly toast—what? We finally agree on a toast to *life* and chuckle softly before we sip and swallow and feel the warmth course its way down. I am aware of sitting next to her, not across a table or moving about in the kitchen. Nor are we speaking of Richard. There is a moment between a man and a woman when they know that something has changed. They have moved from pleasantries, from specificity, from loopy generalities, to the sensory. I know even before I set my snifter on the low table in front of us, even before I turn to look at her—hell, I knew even before I knocked on her front door that her blue eyes and our combined fantasies would lead to this.

Damn, I don't think her eyes could be any larger or any bluer. I'm staring, she's staring, a clock somewhere is ticking, then it chimes as if on cue—beware.

"Seems like I'm sort of here sort of not. Must be the wine," I say. She shrugs. "Long time between *thens* and *nows*, what was and what is." She is still just looking at me. "I'm not making sense, am I?" She shakes her head. "But you know what I mean." She nods. "Well, I'm not that young guy with a flat stomach and a full head of hair, and you're not the young girl I flirted with at Gilson's." She's still looking. "Doesn't matter?" She shakes her head and smiles. "Okay," I say.

I'm following Andrea down the hall; she is almost tiptoeing. When I ask why we're walking on our toes, she looks at me perplexed at first then starts laughing and stomps off and dances up the stairs to the second floor. We're almost to the landing when I miss an exuberant bound, my feet shoot out from under me, and I bounce down about three steps, hit my chin, and lie there full length clawing to keep from further descent. I struggle onto my knees and look up into Andrea's mask of alarm, rubbing my numbed chin. There is a moment of vacuous silence. I'm checking my fingertips to see if there is blood on my chin, and she is watching, a hand held to her mouth.

"Mister suave," I say. "Like my foreplay?"

Andrea gulps and starts laughing so hard she has to bend over. She reaches out and takes my hand; I rise from my blithe humiliation. She examines my chin then very sweetly kisses it, says "All better", and leads me into her bedroom. It is intensely awkward to see this woman, a stranger in every sense were it not for the intersection of our youth, awkward to see her naked and to appear naked before her in my flabby state. She is so white, and where Sylvia (my only comparison) was lithe, Andrea is ample. After taking nervous glimpses of each other we slip between cool sheets and pull the hemmed edge up to our chins. We are synchronized in our modesty. After a moment on the flat of our backs, we turn our heads and smile courteous smiles. Jesus, what am I doing here? This will be a disgraceful moment in this woman's life; there's no way can I satisfy her fantasy. I muster one more smile and think it must appear grossly hypocritical.

"I know," she says. "But it isn't. "Ludicrous. Do you think we are being ludicrous, Edmund? Are you mortified? To be here with me...like this?"

The light from the nightstand on her side creates a cutout of her head. The light from my side is cut in half by my head, drawing a shadow down the middle of her face. I move so that she is fully in a shadow. "Yes," I say, "I'm mortified...but for you. I'm afraid that your expectations come from way back, and I am not that person anymore. I'm...what? Fractured maybe? Yeah, I'm fractured and flawed. You heard me: I'm a derelict."

She rises up on an elbow and looks down into my face. "My, my," she says, "and so poetic you are about your defects. Are you finished? Can we get on with this? As one flawed human to another?"

Andrea Hewitt, the girl from long ago, lays one hand on my chest and with the other she cups my scrotum; she lowers her head and finds my surprised mouth and kisses me hard and squeezes. Holy mother of orgies—so this is the way it should be. It is a shame to discover your naiveté about sexual interplay when you're nearly fifty. What we are experiencing is mutual and equally participatory—she's enjoying this as much as I am; she wants it. Her skin is smooth and yielding, her breath is warm, and she gives low throat sounds of encouragement. When I enter her she is there, she is with me—damn, this is good.

Beneath me, Andrea's legs tense. She shudders and gives out with a dying man's sigh, and that drives me right over the edge, gasping and shaking like a virgin. It's not like I've never gotten my rocks off before, but knowing now that for all those years I was doing it alone is mortifying. I groan and slide off; we're both moist, purring and laughing and spent. It's wonderful.

-13-

Andrea won't get off the phone. We aren't saying anything just now, only listening to each other's breathing. I guess we've said it all, but it's been nice.

"Thought you had some deals to close on," I say.

She sighs. "I do, I really do."

"Okay, you real estate mogul, better get to it. Thanks again for a wonderful evening," I say.

"I *was* nice, wasn't it? Can we do it again?"

"What part did you like best?"

"You are bad," she laughs. "I like bad."

"I noticed." She's still laughing when we disconnect.

It is sort of dull this morning, with no trip to Vernonia. Plus, Tuesday is a long way off, and I've decided not to go out to the nursery today. It's showering outdoors, off and on, and blustery. I can see the one flowering cherry tree we have from my window; it's shedding its blossoms in a hail of white chaff. I'm amused at my impatience, which up until a couple of weeks ago had been lethargy.

I am heating a can of chili for lunch when the Princess tinkles. I yank it off the wall, expecting another computer-generated sales call; a guy says my name as a question.

"Edmund Kirby-Smith?"

"Just Kirby, no Smith," I correct. "Who is this?"

"This is Sid Martin," he says, as if I ought to know. "I'm general manager at Amalgamated-Durant."

"I see." Something flips over in my gut. The chili is starting to bubble; I kill the burner but keep stirring.

"So, Edmund, how are you doing?" The guy's voice is way too smarmy, like the lead-in to a deal on aluminum siding.

"Doing okay," I respond, as flat as I can make it.

"Good, glad to hear it."

"What can I do for you, Mr. Martin?"

"Like I said, I'm with Amalgamated-Durant. You may remember that we bought out Singleton."

"Hard to forget," I say.

"Yes, well, since taking over, we've been busy making the transition and all. Putting in new computers, revamping the coding system to merge with our parent company and, you know, getting up to speed."

"I see." I keep stirring the cooling chili.

"By the way, you people had one sweet operation going here," Sid Martin says. "Yessir, very sweet."

"I know."

"Anyway, the reason I'm calling, Edmund, is to ask…well, we're having a little difficulty with distribution. Nothing big, mind you, but we'd like to smooth things out."

"Uh-huh. What seems to be the problem, something technical?"

Sid Martin laughs. "No, the new computers are working just dandy. It's…to tell you the truth, it's more with the customers."

I'm smiling. My lord this is sweet. "Not sure I follow."

Sounds like the man is gagging, strangling himself on his own laughter. "Customer relations, I guess you'd call it," he says and titters nervously.

"Customer relations."

"Right. Anyway, your name keeps coming up."

"That right."

"Yeah," he says. "A lot of the old Singleton customers remember you, Ed."

"Edmund."

"Huh? Oh, sure, sorry. Anyway, you made a lot of friends when you were here." I don't respond, so he blunders on. "So here's the thing, Edmund. I'd like you to consider coming back to your old job—at a pay increase, of course."

I have to say this brings a warm enema of elation, a pleasant flushing at the pleasure center of my brain that wants to pounce on this moment of vindication. The picture of striding back in triumph has seductive appeal.

"What is it you would like me to do exactly, Mr. Martin?" I ask. "You have all that new technology. Why bring back an old war-horse like me?"

Sid Martin laughs unconvincingly. "Well, I have a young team here," he says. "I just think we can use some wiser heads to balance things."

"You people bought the best little company around, came in beating your breast, scattered us long-timers like straw in the wind," I say, my heart pounding. "You took a chunk of my life and threw it on the scrap heap."

"Look, Edmund, let's not—"

"How about we cut to the chase, Sid," I cut in. "What's really going on here?"

There is a moment of silence on the line. "We're losing customers," Sid Martin says.

"Why is that?"

"I guess we're not treating them right."

"Treating them like numbers, not people?"

"Something like that. Will you come in and talk with me, Edmund?" Sid Martin's bravado has slipped a few notches.

"I'll think about it," I say. "Call you in a couple of days." I take down his number, gently hang up the Princess, and reheat the chili. Tastes great.

———————

I changed my mind about the nursery. I put on a clean tee shirt, jeans, and a pair of old low-top boots I have in the closet and drive out to Manning. A young woman is standing on the nursery's porch peering in. A green mini-van, hers I assume, is sitting in the parking lot, engine running with the driver's door ajar. She rattles the shop's door and knocks and calls out until, in her frustration, she spins and tromps back down the steps right into my path.

"Have you seen Glen? The woman who runs this place?" She seemed more attractive at a distance. Maybe she knows this because she pulls down the sunglasses nestled in her hair and lays them on her nose.

"I just drove up," I say.

The woman swivels; her startlingly white running shoes crunch in the gravel. "She was making me up two custom fuchsia baskets. Promised me they'd be ready." Her intensity drops. "I'm having a yard party tonight, and I had planned on hanging those baskets on the patio. I'm running late, have a million errands. This really irks me."

"I understand," I commiserate. "Let me look around, see if I can find Glen. I'm helping her out some, just started, don't have a key."

"Oh, could you?" Her eyebrows rise hopefully; she even puts her dark glasses back up in her hair and tries seducing me with a toothy smile. A clot of lipstick on one of her incisors diminishes the appeal.

The gate to the nursery yard is padlocked, so I edge around the fence and slog through weeds and brush to the rear of the property and make my way in. I find Glen in a little office off the back loading dock, asleep, head resting on folded arms atop a cluttered desk. The sweet smell of alcohol meets my nostrils before I see the empty Wild Turkey bottle. When I shake her by the arm, all I get is heavier breathing; I can't rouse her. With the big brimmed hat off, she seems less formidable. Her brown hair is pulled back in a rubber-banded ponytail, and her face is calmed by inebriated slumber. The two fuchsia baskets are sitting on the dock. The woman is ecstatic and hands me four twenties when I don't know the price.

Glen is still unconscious. I shake her more vigorously, but all I get is a snort and more heavy breathing. Damn, it is so easy to get sucked into the lives of other people and—just like that—be handed a share of their baggage. I wander out onto the loading dock then come back and shake Glen one more time before locking the place up. I'm gone.

The Chevelle is idling in a throaty hum, and I'm sitting with my arm on the sill of the open window and staring. I can't do it. It isn't *my* drunken stupor or *my* business that's being neglected, but some throwback old-dog habit bubbles up. I rummage around and find a key to the front door and go about setting merchandise out on the porch. I arrange it like I know what I'm doing: stacks of clay pots, a rack of garden tools, handmade planter boxes, and bags of potting mix. I prop the door open and nose around behind the counter, discover a yellowed price sheet taped to the counter with masking tape and a drawer with change in it: seven ones, a couple of fives, and an assortment of coins—maybe enough to get by. I'm in the process of selling a cedar bird feeder and a bag of birdseed to an elderly woman when Glen appears from the back and leans in the doorway. Her hat's back on, eyes are slits, and she's studying me with the look of a loan shark—and I'm overdue.

"There you are, Glen," the old lady says.

Glen raises a hand but doesn't smile. "Alberta," she says.

"See you got some help," the old woman says.

"It would seem."

"And about time." I get a smile from the woman, and she departs to feed her feathered moochers.

Glen Wood straightens up, puts her hands in her pants pockets, and we stare at one another. After a moment, I step over and hold out the key and drop it into her open hand when she reaches out. She keeps staring at me the whole time. I tell her the woman came by for the fuchsia baskets and gave me eighty bucks. "Owed me fifty each," is the reply, "Custom job". I shrug and turn to leave. She is on the porch looking out at me when I start the Chevelle; it's like I'm looking at a child whom I am about to abandon. But I do anyway. I've been around that bend before. His name was Uncle Skip, except he never skipped a day without being a happy drunk. My mother's grief over her little brother ate years off of her life. Uncle Skip sobered up for her funeral.

I get a burger to go at the Dairy Queen and drive back to Portland arguing with myself about Glen Wood. Damn it, anyway. I came through Manning for one purpose: to find Richard Vickerman and see if his principles were a young man's myth or truth. Glen Wood was a drunk before I happened by. So if I go back to the nursery it will be because I think Glen Wood needs me. And won't I be special?

113

-14-

Tuesday is here again. My sister calls while I'm eating a toast-and-fried-egg sandwich for breakfast. She wants to invite me over for dinner tonight.

"Salty'll barbecue some steaks," she says. "It will be fun."

"Need a rain check," I say.

"Oh?" she responds. "What, you have a hot date?"

"I'm following up on your suggestion," I say.

"What suggestion?"

"To look up my past. Remember?"

"No, I don't. Wait, you mean about that guy, Dick?"

"Dick Vic. Richard Vickerman. I've been looking for him ever since."

"Really!" Her voice rises. "No kidding. Did you find him?"

"Almost, plus his daughter."

"His daughter," she says with innuendo. "Something I should know?"

"There is nothing I can tell you."

"That sounds suspicious. So Edmund, you *do* sound better. Are you?"

"Could be. We'll see," I answer. "Oh, I have a sort of job now, too. Sorry, got to run now." I hang up while Sugar is saying something I don't make out. Later, Sis.

A little after ten o'clock I'm in Vernonia, cruising down Bridge Street and wondering if this will be another dry run. I nose the Chevelle up Texas and onto Mississippi Avenue and park behind the orange Pinto, sort of expecting to see Twyla on the front porch in her chair sucking on another Virginia Slim. She's not, but the Honda's there. I swing the car door open and stand in the wedge, one elbow on the doorframe the other on the roof, and shake a kink out of my right leg. I'm almost to the porch when I hear the cough. He's standing in the shadow of a cedar tree, staring at me from under the brim of an unruly fedora.

"Richard?" I squint his way. The man is tall like Richard Vickerman, but the similarity ends there. This person is gaunt and ashen and stooped. He's older, I expected that, but not this version. I plaster on a smile and edge forward. He steps back at my approach, and when I extend my hand it hangs in mid air, unmet. "It's me. Edmund. Edmund Kirby."

Through sunken slits he studies me like I'm a government agent. The trademark mustache is gone and so is the perpetual smile. I lower my hand, try to keep my smile up, and nod like I know something.

"Must be at least twenty-five years, more than that, likely," I say. "You're a hard man to find."

He starts to speak but begins coughing instead. He pulls out a clotted handkerchief, hacks into it after the coughing spasm, and shoves it back into the pocket of his bib overalls.

"Don't want you comin' around here anymore." His voice has a familiar tone, but it's raspy. With each breath his chest rises, filled with the trapped scourge of emphysema, and with each cough there are gurgles of infected phlegm.

"Come on, you mean Dick Vic won't sit down with an old friend for a visit?"

Nothing, just staring with eyes that study me out of those narrow crevices.

"Don't want to talk? How about if I reminisce, you listen? No? I could chat with Twyla about the old days, and you could sit with us."

He turns from me and moves away slowly toward the back of the house like he has to invent each step. I holler out, "We could smile in the face of adversity." With that he stops, his breathing labored, and turns and glares at me. At least, I think that is what he's doing; I can't quite tell. Or maybe he is considering. I don't know, but he moves on and disappears around the corner of the house. I debate going after him but decide against that and sit on the hood of the Honda. After a bit, Twyla comes out the front door and down the steps. She lights a cigarette and turns her head to exhale the smoke away from me.

"Wouldn't talk," I say. "I don't get it."

"Didn't say anything?"

"Well yeah: not to come around anymore."

Twyla blows more smoke out and shrugs. "Been tryin' to tell you. He gave you the kiss-off, that's what he done. Guess that's it, then."

"No, I'm not buying this. I'll be back next week."

Her face darkens, and she starts to say something then stops and flicks the ash off her cigarette.

"How is he?" I ask. "Seems pretty bad to me."

"Oh, this is a sort of regular day. Like I say, he's dying, and it's one damnation of a disease. Suffocates you to death." She sucks on the cigarette.

"How about you? Thinking on quitting?"

She drops the butt and steps on it. "Hell, always thinking about quitting."

"Should I write him another note? Does he read them?"

She purses her lips. "If you want. I'll give it to him, all I can

116

promise. Maybe he reads 'em. I don't know. Seems like a waste of time to me, but…whatever."

Richard, It was good to see you. You know what this is all about, don't you? It's about the man you were and what you stood for and how that impacted my life. May not mean much to you, but it does to me. So I'm not quitting. See you next Tuesday. Edmund

I slow down on the way through Manning and look in at the nursery. It is open, and there are two cars in the parking lot. For an instant I consider pulling off, but I don't.

You know how they say things come in threes? I mean significant things. I figure that call from Sid Martin about my old job, that was one. I was hoping by now that Dick Vic opening up to me would have been the first. Anyway, I'm barely in the door from Vernonia, when the phone rings. I'm getting more calls in a week than I got in three months before. I don't even jump anymore. It's my daughter, Samantha, surprise, surprise. I hadn't even thought of the "threes-thing" though, until her call—her contact has been that rare.

And I get no snide or smirky overtones, just, "Hey, Dad, how's it going?"

"Oh it's going," I say cautiously. "And you guys?"

"Good. We're good. Sorry I haven't called more or invited you over for dinner or something. It's just been, you know, so hectic. But we'll have to do that, have you over. Phil could barbecue steaks or something." My second barbecued steak offer of the week.

"That'd be nice." I'm cruising here, wondering.

"Yeah, we'll do it," she says. I don't jump in; I decide to wait her out until she spills whatever it is. "So, you ever hear anything from Mom?" she says finally.

There it is.

"Not a word," I say. "Of course, I wouldn't expect to, Sam.

117

What's over is over. That's the way it is when a man and woman call it quits."

"Yeah, I suppose so. Not always, though. A friend of mine, her parents were divorced then got back together after a year or so. Got married again. Really neat. Everybody, the whole family, is happy, you know."

"Uh-huh." A chill runs up the back of my legs.

"So it can happen. Dad?" Her voice goes up.

"Yeah?" Here it comes.

"Mom and I have been talking. I keep in touch. Pretty regularly. We talk usually once a week."

"That's good. How's she doing?"

"Well...hold on a second." Her voice is muffled. "I'm on the phone...with Dad. Sorry, where was I? Oh yeah, Mom." Another pause. "Well, that's why I'm calling. It's just that...how do I say this? I don't know...I..."

"What is it, Sam? She sick or something?"

"No. Least not *sick* sick."

"Uh-huh." I hold the phone with my neck and shoulder, reach into the fridge for a beer, shut the door with a hip move, and pull the tab open on the can—I'm listening.

"Dad, you there?"

"Yeah. So you say she's not *sick* sick. That mean she's unsick?" I chuckle and take a swallow of beer.

"Come on, Dad, I'm being serious here. Could you for once... I'm sorry, it's just that...well, she's really unhappy."

Sylvia's unhappy. Golly gee. "Well, happiness is a relative state, Sam. You calling me about your mom having a bad hair day? She doesn't like the traffic in Seattle?"

I can hear my daughter suck in an agitated breath. "I don't know why I'm doing this. Look she...here's the thing: she thinks she's made a mistake."

"What, on her taxes? What is this?"

118

"Geez, Dad, get a clue. I'm talking about your divorce."

I'm glued to the floor, the can of beer clamped in my hand. I can't be hearing what I'm hearing.

"Phil, I'm still on the phone." Samantha is almost yelling.

"Okay, Dad, sorry. So you get what I'm saying, right?"

I hold the phone hard against my ear and take another drink from the can. "Yeah, think I get it. The woman who lived through years and years of an empty-calories marriage wants to go back on the old diet. Isn't that what you called it, Sam? Zero-calories marriage."

"I was joking."

"I don't think so."

"Dad. Anyway, this is between you two. Will you talk to her?"

"About us getting back together?"

"I don't know, I...Mom's real sad. I feel bad for her."

"Sam, you told me she'd made the right decision leaving me. Right?"

Samantha takes a couple of deep breaths. "Dad, I know what I said. But this is different. It's not my call, anyway. It's Mom's."

"Different? I don't get it. The woman I lived with and loved for twenty-seven years then rips my life to shreds. She's not happy now and wants to go back to Mister Excitement here?"

"I knew this wouldn't work. She made the right choice getting divorced in the first place—like I said before. Sorry I even called you."

The connection is guillotined. Guess old Phil won't be cooking up those steaks anytime soon. I try to imagine what it would be like to slide into bed next to Sylvia again. Damn that's funny; then again, sad, too.

When I finish telling Felix about my daughter's phone call, he erupts in a convulsion of laughter. We're sitting out on his balcony, drinking the usual. It's rare to get a real guffaw out of

Felix, you know, a real belly laugh. This time the guy is nearly jubilant.

"And just when I'd about given up on the day," he says. He offers me another beer out of his cooler. "That's almost as good as the day the garbage kid dumped the drop box. Could hardly breathe from laughing that time, watching the guy squatting in the chicken bones, cantaloupe rinds and putrid diapers. But this, this is way beyond that. This is part of the human comedy. Woman thinks she'd be coming back to the same-o same-o?"

His laughing at my ex-wife goes down crooked and pricks the bubble of happy revenge that I'd been floating in since Samantha's call. I leave Felix savoring the sweet and sour of my life, go back to my apartment, and sit in the dark. I think of Sylvia and remember throwing all her photographs away; I burned the damn things really, tore them into bits and burned them in the sink right over there. Rinsed her ashes down the drain.

Now I can't think of her clearly anymore. When I try to, I'm like a kid who's spun around and around and can't make sense of where he is, eyes wide open but in la-la land. My recent past is like that, mostly the part about Sylvia—all out of whack. A sudden chill hits me. What will I do if she calls and wants to talk about rewinding our lives and starting back from before last Memorial Day? No harm no foul?

Poor Sylvia, she thought she was going to plow new ground when she sashayed out of my life. All she did was fall into the conga line with the half that goes splits-ville every year.

Hey, Sylvia, I'm not me anymore—not that *me*, anyway.

———

Andrea calls late, around ten. I'm on my back watching *Law and Order* in glorious green and orange. She wants to know if I saw her dad today. When I tell her that I did, I hear her breath suck in.

"Edmund," she's put out, "why didn't you call me?"

"I'm sorry, you're right," I say. "Brain dead on this end, I guess."

She is quiet for a moment. "Did you mention me?" she asks.

"No, barely got my own name out."

"How was he? How'd he look?"

"Like hell. He's dying, can barely breathe, and Twyla says it's getting worse. I want to reach him before he's out of it."

"Maybe you're being too patient. Make him talk. I want to see him before he dies too, Edmund."

"Yeah, let's make sure we get a crack at him before he goes. Right? You and me? Then it's okay for him to check out."

She doesn't say anything.

"Sorry," I say.

"Yeah."

"By the way, you'll never guess," I say, after an uncomfortable silence.

"What?"

"Sylvia thinks she made a mistake. Divorcing the man here."

"You mean she wants to get back together...with you?"

"It would seem so," I answer.

"Well," she says, "I guess it happens. Would you consider it?"

"As the wicked witch said, *Something's brewing*. But it won't be this kid."

She laughs. "You were together a long time, though."

"I was in a trance. I'm awake now."

"That would be strange," she says. "Can't imagine me getting back together with Cliff."

"You know," I say, "that's the first time you've ever said his name—your ex's. Cliff, Hewitt, right?"

"Don't remind me. There are reasons I don't talk about back then...and him."

"How would you react if you got a call from him suggesting you talk about getting back together?"

"Gawd! Pack my bags and go into a witness protection program." She hesitates then asks, "What about you? If she calls... Sylvia? I know you joked, but what would you do, really?"

"Been thinking about that," I answer, "since my daughter called. You can't go back, can you?"

"Back to what, a former spouse?" She laughs. "I'm the wrong girl to answer that one. No way X-ray."

"What?"

"Something we said as kids, means absolutely not, mister. How can you? All of those insults and hurtful truths."

"Hurtful truths?"

"Yes," she says. "Everything from toilet behavior to social inadequacies; how do you take those back?"

"Or having to live a life of empty calories," I add.

"What's that mean?"

"No idea, but it was the life Sylvia had to live with me, I guess."

Andrea laughs. "I could use more empty calories."

"I can give you all you want."

"Can't wait."

-15-

The next morning, I sleep in until nine, shower, have cereal and bananas, then run the Chevelle down on Lombard and fill it up with super. I splurge on a car wash, one of those where you use a high-pressure wand; I dry the car with an old bath towel, and she really shines. I stop by Safeway on the way home, pick up a few things and am back at the apartment parking lot by eleven fifteen. I put the blue tarp over the car—now what?

My life has taken on momentum that has been missing for months, and I'm not quite sure how to react to it. I now have a list in my head of things to do and people to see, or not—that's all been missing. From wanting to sit down face-to-face with Richard to deciding if I really want to sit down face-to-face with Sid Martin of Amalgamated-Durant to paralyzed at the thought of sitting down face-to-face with Sylvia, I'm like a man walking on ice. There are several hands being held out—which one should I take?

I let the rest of the day sort of slide by, watch a little television, and page through my grandfather's stamp album. Dinner is a tuna sandwich and a cold beer. I'm dining at the kitchen table when someone taps at my door. I ignore the first two knocks, figuring it's probably some kid with a stud through one nostril grinning like we're old buds, wanting money for Greenpeace.

The blows to the door intensify, so I yank it open on the fourth wallop. It's Sylvia.

"Edmund!" she blurts out.

I've gotten bigger; she's gotten leaner. She's dressed to kill in a pair of silky green slacks, a matching jacket, a white scoop-necked blouse underneath, and black heels. I'm dressed casually—tee-shirt, sweat pants, and slippers. Under the entry light I see the dark circles under her eyes. I step back, chewing a ball of tuna and white bread; and she walks in like she belongs, pushing in a cloud of woodsy perfume. She pivots, in complete control, and stands in the live-in kitchen, clasping her hands at her waist. She watches me close the door.

I put my half-full beer can on the counter, turn back, and run my tongue over my teeth, clearing any tuna remnants. Sylvia slowly turns her head one way then the next, taking in the sumptuousness of my abode.

"I tried to call," she says, still evaluating the place.

"Really?" I say. "Must have been out."

"I called three times," she refutes.

I laugh. "Must have been out three times. I don't have a message machine."

"I know. May I?" she asks, gesturing.

"Sure, have a seat."

She goes to the couch, sits gracefully, and looks at me. "How are you?"

I shrug. "You can see I'm living grand."

She blinks, deflecting my sarcasm, and runs a hand over the leg of her shimmery slacks, flicking at something she doesn't want there. "It's cozy," she says.

"It is that. So, how's Seattle?" I ask.

"It's fine," she says. "Too much traffic, but fine."

"Sandra and Bill?"

"They're fine."

I nod and swallow. "So, you come down to see Samantha?"
She crosses a leg. "No," she says calmly. "I came to see you."
I fold my arms across my chest and curse to myself. "Oh?"
"Sam said she called you."
"She did." I respond as blandly as I can. "Yesterday."
"Then you know."
I clear my throat, stalling. "I'm not sure. It was a little confusing. Something about you not being happy up there." I pause. "In Seattle."

Sylvia is looking at me like she used to when she was tired of me. It's a bored stare, and she doesn't blink for a long time. Her manikin state. "That's what she told you? Really?"

My scalp itches. I scratch at it and say, "Well, she said you were having second thoughts or something."

"Does that surprise you, Edmund?"

"Mildly put," I say. "Astounded is more like it."

"Yes, well I'm amazed myself." Her laugh is strained. "Go figure."

I bob my head and look down at my feet.

"It's a…it's been different than I thought," she says.

"Different?" My eyebrows go up.

She starts to say something but stops and brings a hand to her mouth and begins to cry, her body shaking, eyes closed. I drop my hands to my side and wonder when she will take in a breath. At last she does—gasping then sobbing again.

"I'm miserable, Edmund." The words are squeezed out in spasms of breath taking and a resurgence of crying. I tear off a paper towel and hand it to her. She blows her nose, folds the towel, and dabs at her tears.

What the hell am I supposed to say? I know what I want to say: *tough titty*. I'm getting a certain amount of enjoyment out of this, pathetic as it is. Should I fall on my sword and beg her to return? *Look around you, Sylvia*, I'm thinking. *Look at where I am and why.*

"Well," I say, "misery comes with the territory. That's the way it is, I guess."

Sylvia sniffs, wipes her nose, and blinks at me, a curious expression on her face. "But do we have to be?" she says. "Miserable?"

I shrug. "Can't think of a way not to be. Unless we both had ended up with plenty of money and new lovers that made us moan. Other than that, misery's the name of the game."

She tries to laugh and wipes at her rosy nose. "You've become quite the cynic," she says and gets up from the couch. "I used to be the woman of your dreams, didn't I?" She comes right up to me and puts an open hand on my chest. "Didn't I?" she says again and rubs me in a circular motion. "Used to be like that in the back seat of your Plymouth."

"Nash," I say.

She looks confused.

"It was a Nash. Had fold-down seats," I say. "Remember?"

She forces a smile. "Oh yes, the Nash. I'd forgotten."

The old Sylvia found me uncouth whenever I mentioned those youthful carnal episodes. I guess it's okay now.

Her perfume is tickling my nose. I squeeze my nostrils and exhale. "That was a long time ago, and we were kids," I say. "A hard dick and a wet pussy passed for true love back then. Hormones is all it was."

"Ooh, vulgar now." She leans against me. "I like that. The new Edmund."

When her other hand reaches between my legs I quit breathing for an instant and grunt my surprise. She begins to rub and squeeze. I jump and step away. "What the hell, Sylvia?" Then she is pressing her face into mine, kissing me and trying to run her tongue past my lips and into my mouth. I take her by the shoulders and push her back.

"Come on," she says, her voice strained, desperate. "I want you."

126

"No." I flex my shoulders. "You don't want me. I don't know what you want, but you don't want me."

She steps away awkwardly, moves back to the couch, and sits down. She leans forward on her knees and puts her hands together beneath her chin, prayerlike. "What happened to us?" she says.

"Hell, how should I know?" I answer. "I'm just the one that got the letter."

She looks over at me. "I'm sorry how that was done."

I grunt. "Out of the blue. Laid me out, I tell you. Still don't know why. All you said was something about saving yourself. From whom—me?"

"No."

"From what, then?"

She sighs. "From us."

"I'm confused," I say.

"We never had a chance, you know. Didn't you feel that way? That we just did the right thing and kept on going. You felt that too, didn't you?"

I nod. "Sure."

"Trapped, we were trapped. You never got to finish college," she says. "And I...I never got to try anything."

"Hell, Syl, millions of people don't get to live their dreams. Most of us, I'd guess."

She bobs her head. "I know that now. Guess I've known it forever. I'm not a child. I just had a childish moment." She pauses and sits back. "We did care for one another, didn't we, Edmund? Once?"

"Of course," I say. "I'll always care about you...in some way."

She laughs lightly. "*In some* way. What's that mean?"

"I don't know. I guess it means that we had something, but we've moved on to another phase of our lives."

"Phase," she says. "That's a strange word to use. Can this new phase include both of us?"

"You mean us together?"

"Uh-huh."

"I didn't mean that," I say.

"Do you have someone…in your life?"

"I don't know," I answer. "Maybe."

She suddenly stands. "So all this *we had something once* is your way of saying there's no hope for us again."

"Sylvia."

"Samantha, she told you that I was open to reconciling, didn't she?"

"Not in those words, she—"

"Damn you, Edmund." She looks around the room. "And so here you live in this…this place."

I smile. "This is what I have left after you had your childish moment…you and Singleton. They want me back, too."

Sylvia's eyes are full and open; she's exploring my face like it's an unappealing painting. "So are you?"

"What, going back there? I don't know, thinking it over. Probably not." I look at her. "Wouldn't make any difference for us, I don't think."

"So what will you do?" she asks.

"I'm doing it." I smile. "Still think you want me, Syl?" I raise my arms. "There's more of me to love. The old Edmund was too staid and predictable? Here's the new me."

Sylvia raises a hand to her mouth and gapes at me.

"Not the man of your dreams after all, Sylvia? You want to go back to the robotic life on the cul-de-sac? Gone, baby, gone, gone, gone—thanks to you."

That's pretty much how it ends. After a bout of choking and tears, my ex-wife, the woman who lusted after me until I confirmed my severely limited future, stumbles out of my apartment and likely my life—for good, I would assume. I'm rooted to the same spot, staring at nothing, when she slings the door back open and stands framed in the opening, one hand clutching the doorknob and the other jabbing the air with a red-nailed forefinger.

Her voice vibrates with rage, "I don't know what I was thinking, coming here, throwing myself at you."

"I know why." I step toward her, my knees quivering, flooded with the juices of payback. "Life was just there for you. We weren't rolling in it, but I was the only one carrying a lunch bucket. The dull worker bee—that was me."

Sylvia's face twisted into such a snarl I thought she was going to roar or howl. "You don't think I worked? You ass. Running that house was a life sentence, looking at you scratching, washing out your skid marks—I put up with all your disgusting ways. I suffered the most tedious, monotonous life imaginable. Twenty-five years with you, Edmund, the most bloodless man to walk upright. Absolute torture, a slow death."

"Twenty-seven," I say.

"What?"

"We were married twenty-seven memorable years," I correct. "Remember?"

"Don't remind me."

"Five minutes ago you wanted me." I move closer; she steps back. "You wanted me!" I'm yelling, my hands balled into fists.

"I don't want you."

"Oh really?" my voice is trembling. "Then why in the fuck are you here? We know why, don't we?" We stare at each other, hyperventilating. "The money's gone, isn't it, Syl? That's it. Or nearly gone. And you're in a panic. Right?"

"All right. Yes. Why else would I even consider living with you…god, sleeping with you, letting you touch me again? The thought of it." She cringes.

"So earn your own way in life for once," I say with glee. "Or go stick your tongue down some other poor slob's throat. Has to be a lotta guys who'd sell their souls to live with a bitch like you. Just not this one."

Tears of anger, desperate tears, spill down Sylvia's face. She flings an arm out, gesturing. "So live in this…this hole, if you can call this living. I feel so much better now. I'll be able to re-call my last image of you existing in this box with your breath stinking of fish."

The door crashes shut. I wait for her to barge back in again, but she doesn't. The only sound is the copier repair guy who lives next door pounding on his wall. He wants a little peace. My body is shuddering as I stand at the sink and rinse out the empty tuna can, heart beating, nerves twitching from the throes of the shouting match Sylvia and I had avoided during the divorce— the rage we both had wanted to spew at each other. By the time my coffee finishes spurting and hissing into the pot, I have calmed down. For several minutes, I lean on the kitchen counter and heave the sobs I never did when I should have. A piece of my life has been excised; the surgery was painful.

-16-

It's about ten by the time I get to the nursery the next morning, and it has begun to sprinkle. I ease the Chevelle off the highway, drift onto the lot and crunch to a stop. Glen is squatting next to a potted plant on the porch of the shop, waiting on a pudgy bald-headed man; she spots me as soon as I emerge from the car. The man is focused on the adolescent sprig of a young tree rooted in a black plastic tub. He's chattering and fingering the leaves while Glen peers out at me from under her straw hat and nods as if she's listening. I lean on the fender of the car, getting my rump wet in the process, and wait until the man waddles to his SUV, lugging his potted prize. He looks even less earthy than I do—the tree's bound to die.

There are several other cars on the lot, and through the open gate to the yard I can see people wandering about among the nursery stock. Glen ignores them and ambles over. There is a fine mist in the air; I can feel it dampening the shoulders of my shirt and wetting down my thin hair and my scalp.

When she approaches, I stand away from the car and swipe at the dampness on my seat. "April showers bring customers," I say. It doesn't rhyme, but what the heck; I'm swimming for an opening line.

She brushes her hands together in a cleansing motion. "What're you doing here?" Her eyes are moving, exploring.

"Nice to see you, too," I respond, smiling.

"Didn't figure you'd be back."

"Yeah, well, there you go. Figuring out folks is a pitiful waste of time. That's what I've discovered, anyway."

Glen looks over her shoulder and back in a slow, relaxed motion. "You'd be wanting an explanation."

"Nope. Wondering what'd you'd think of hiring a man back on after he walked off the job. Any chance?"

The mist is still coming down. I wipe away the drop that is forming on the end of my nose. Glen hesitates, studies me from inside her weathered face. "There's a dry shirt hanging in my office. Behind the door."

By the time I find the faded blue chambray shirt and dry off, the sun has broken through, and the mist is gone. I roll the sleeves up past my elbows and go where Glen points, helping customers, mainly carrying purchases to cars and handling simple sales and sending people to Glen with their earthy questions. When there is a lull between customers, she puts me to work moving plastic bags of mulch and planting mix, sweeping the store—tasks within my skill range. At five o'clock on the nose, she has me padlock the gate while she turns the Open sign to its Closed side and twists the dead bolt on the shop door. We're closed. Glen scoops the checks, credit card slips, and most of the bills out of the cash box, leaves enough to make change, and strides out the back door. I follow in her wake; and we end up in the cramped storage-room office, where she peels off the straw hat, hangs it on a hook by the door without looking, and drops onto the bentwood armed chair at her desk. She thumbs through the day's take then stuffs it all into the middle drawer.

"Good day?" I ask.

"Seen worse. Spring's the thing 'round here. Weren't for people itching to dig their pinkies in the dirt, I'd be bagging groceries somewhere." In a move that stands me up from leaning in the doorway, she pulls a bottle out of the bottom desk drawer. "Snort?" When I don't respond she throws off a staccato burst of laughter, high clicking sounds. "Should see the look on your face." She twists the cap off the bottle and reaches for a water glass sitting next to the phone. "Get one thing clear for certain here," she says. "This here's my place. Run it the way I want. Same with my life. Having a drink of some good sour mash is something I enjoy, 'specially after a day's labor." She pours the glass half full and takes a swallow and leans back.

"Sure?" she says. I shrug and watch her rummage a glass out of the bottom drawer and hold it up to the light. "Clean enough. Pour your poison."

I'm not partial to bourbon, but right then its bite jukes my tired blood. Glen kicks off her heavy leather clogs, puts her socked feet up on the desk, and raises her glass.

"Salud." We drink again. "Sit, damn it," she says. "Makes my neck ache looking up that way." With one arm she pulls a low stool from out of the cramped corner behind her and pushes it at me.

I sit and take another sip from my glass. A squint is puckering the edges of her eyes. She drinks some more from her glass. "You don't talk much," she says. "I like that."

"Caught me on a good day. Usually, I'm a motormouth."

"Hmm, let's hope not. Talkin' don't leave time for thinking, sleeping, or drinking. The time left over is for making do. When yer yapping, nothing's happening, so I'll make this quick. Number one: Why'd you come back? Number two: What're you doing here in the first place?"

I reach out and sit my glass on the corner of the desk. "Number one," I tap my left forefinger with my right, "Don't have a clue. Number two," I tap again, "I'm in between."

Glen throws her head back, empties the glass, then clunks it down. "Number one," she taps a finger, "is pity. Number two, between what and what?"

"No, number one is guilt," I say. "Number two, between life part one and part two."

"Ha, guilt," she says. "Over me? You know what guilt is? It's pity all dressed up. Pity I don't need. Don't want none, either. Makes my teeth grind. Been running this dirt pile for twelve years on my own, ever since my dick-for-brains husband departed middle of the night. Swoosh. Gone, so long. And that's all right .I'll kill him if he crosses the property line again. Pitchfork through his pump."

"So there's no one else to help run this place?" I ask.

Glen squints. "You mean like kids and such? Thank the gods my man and I never managed to conceive. Besides, why do you think I had that Help Wanted sign out?"

I tip my glass up and shrug. "Guess you're as cut off as me, then."

She sweeps an arm through the air. "Oh, I got a father off somewhere in Texas and a sort-of sister living not far from here."

"What's a *sort-of* sister?"

"Stepsister," she says, shaking her head. "Older. Piece of work, she is. Mean as a stepped-on rattler. Between her nastiness and being kicked around by my father, I came out tough as jerky." She takes another swig. "Had to be."

I just look at her and hold my tongue. There is nothing riskier than commenting on someone else's kin.

"Well, never mind all that," she says and takes another swallow of bourbon. "What's your name again? Know it's Ed something 'er other. Give me the whole thing."

"Edmund J. Kirby."

"What's the J for?"

"Joyce."

"You don't say? Bet you kept that one under wraps growing up."

134

"My mother had a thing for Joyce Kilmer. Poet?"

"Hell, yes. Ain't nothing like a tree. Fits right in 'round here, don't it? Nuther?" She lifts the bottle, I hold my glass out, and she pours me too much. "So you said you're between life parts one and two? What's that all about?" She looks at me with those black marble eyes.

I toss back a big one and hold my breath while it scorches its way down. By the time we've knocked off the bourbon, I've told her most everything, and I'm sick—rolling-gut sick. Glen is only nominally drunk, but then, she's experienced. I feel her wiry strength when she helps me up, grunting and cursing at me to do my part. She lays my left arm across her back and guides me, stumbling down the stairs and wobbling around and through the trees and shrubs and planting beds to the back of the yard where a single-wide trailer sits concealed behind a row of mature arborvitae. She props me against the trailer's metal siding while she opens the door, but before she can get back to me I slump over and vomit into a cedar planter box with some kind of as-tonished plant in it.

Glen stands over me without a word of encouragement and calmly paces beside me; I smell cigarette smoke. Thanks for the sympathy. When I have retched all I have to retch, she grabs me under the arms, mutters at me to stand up, grips the back of my belt, and propels me and my flailing arms and loopy legs up into the trailer, where I'm dropped onto something that bounces back. Oh, please. My stomach reels, and I pray for calm just before the mush in my head smothers my consciousness.

I awake, still face down, my mouth open and a pain in my hip. The only thing that rings with familiarity is the aroma of coffee. If one can be described as a bag of cow chips, that's me. And I move like one, scooting up and propping myself on one elbow, blinking through waxed-paper eyes and licking at the dried spittle on my lips. Glen speaks. I know it is her; I just can't see too well. She welcomes me to the land of the living and points me in the direction of a compact bathroom. I rinse my face and my eyes, and in the mirror I make out a round indentation in my right cheek from something I slept on, maybe an upholstery button. I cup water into my mouth with one hand and wash out a foul aftertaste as best I can.

Glen is holding out a cup when I slowly carom into her cramped kitchen.

"Welcome to Bourbon Street," she says. I manage a weak smile and suck up the hot brown liquid with gratitude. My empty stomach wobbles when the unadulterated caffeine hits. I wince and grunt and grab for the piece of dry toast Glen is holding out. She's been there. I slide onto an upholstered bench seat in the dining nook, lean on my elbows, and chew and swallow and wait for the waves to subside.

"Bourbon's not your drink," Glen says. My smile is limp and I'm thinking: *What clued you?* And why is she looking fit enough to throw me ten yards? Her hair is tied back, eyes are bright, and sleeves are rolled up on a red flannel shirt; you'd think she had been drinking spring water. She talks me into eating a couple of eggs and having some orange juice. She makes a new man of me; at least I can breathe on my own and stand without reeling.

Glen has dried my shirt. I change in her bedroom, wash my face, damp comb my hair, and come out looking nearly okay. She hands me forty bucks. When I raise my eyebrows, she says, "Off the books. Consider I'm training you, anyhow. So it's like a scholarship, not real pay."

I look at the two bills in my hand, laugh, and shrug. I'm at the door when she says, "By the way, don't expect me to treat you to my best booze regular now. Drop by when you can."

I nod, ease down the trailer steps, and test my equilibrium on solid ground.

The Chevelle runs throaty and smooth on the drive back into Portland. The sun is out again. I've tuned in the jazz station and am cruising along with the window down, mulling over the sudden eruption of crazy episodes in my life, when a couple of kids in a Mazda, one lowered and flashing shiny mag wheels, come alongside me just south of North Plains. The kid driving revs the sewing-machine engine and gets some racket out of an echo can attached to the tailpipe. He tromps on it, speeds ahead, and drops, back taunting me. I smile and shake them off. But when the kid on the passenger side yells something about *old man* and *chicken shit* and gives me the finger, I change my mind and punch it. The Quadra Jet four-barrel carburetor kicks in, sucks air like an elephant having sex, and 396 cubic inches shove me back in the seat. And we teach two kids what real muscle is. At ninety I get off the accelerator and wind down to sixty. When the Mazda passes, the two kids are hunkered down, staring straight ahead, not knowing that they just got their asses kicked by a grown-up who is less credible than two airhead teenage males. Was a silly ass thing to do—no insurance, expired license—but it felt good.

Felix is out making the circuit when I get back to the apartment. He's on the other side of the quadrangle, moving like he's in a freeze frame. I sit on our memorial bench, feel the late morning sun warm my face and chest, and wait him out; he takes his time.

"You look like hell hath no fury," he says when he finally arrives. He steps on the butt of the cigarillo he's been smoking and drops his big rump down beside me. "Pinkest whites I ever seen. Story to go with 'em?"

I knuckle my eyes. "Bottle of bourbon, a woman, and her trailer."

"Sounds promising."

"Heaving in her planter box might be a setback."

"Depends. You sleep over?"

"In a manner of speaking."

"Not a setback," he says. "Speaking of women, your ex ever made contact?"

"She came by, actually," I answer. "Tried to seduce me. No—swear to god—she had a grip on my gonads, and her tongue was trying to reach my epiglottis."

"Sounds like a Hallmark moment."

"One in a series," I say. "I even got a call from my old company. The new management wants me to come back."

"That right? You gonna do it?"

"Hell, I don't know. Besides, I already have a new job." When he does a head jerk, I say, "Guess I forgot to tell you. That planter I threw up in? Belongs to a woman who owns a little nursery in Manning. I'm doing some part-time work for her."

"Manning? Where the hell's that?"

"On the way to Vernonia." Felix turns his head and squints at me. "It's a long story," I add.

"Must be." He leans back, lights up another cigarillo, and takes a drag. Smoke curls out of his nose. "You're raising a big cloud of dust all of a sudden. Thought this was all about finding that fella Richard. How's that coming?"

"I'm getting there."

"You know me," he says. "Not into rushing a thing. Besides that, it goes against the grain to be nosing in on another man's business. But this is slower than five o'clock on I-5 north."

"Is the leader of languor setting me a time limit?" I say.

Felix snorts and flicks his half-smoked little cigar out into the grass. We watch it smolder. "I found Stoddard, looked him in the eye, got my answer, and was outta there." He leans over on his knees. "Gotta be that way, as I see it. Otherwise...well, it's like them Lilliputians, in *Gulliver's Travels*?" I frown and shrug. "These things that have been happening to you...since you went looking for this guy? You're just like old Gulliver. These Lilliputians have you tied down, and I can see these little ropes hanging all over you."

I chuckle. "What are you talking about?"

"Laugh if you want. Go ahead. I'm just saying you're lettin' too many players in the game." He pauses, pulls out a wadded handkerchief, and honks into it twice. "None of my business, but gonna say it anyway. Kick the door in. Get eyeball to eyeball with old Richard: ask the questions, ask for forgiveness, spit in his eye, kiss him—whatever you planned on doing—and get outta there."

"It's different for you," I sass. "Your guy was locked up where you could get to him."

"Still had to kick the door in," he says, pushes up off the bench, and toddles off.

-17-

I sleep the sleep of Gulliver, dreaming of ropes and having my body restrained. The ropes are wrapped around their hands and they smile and pull: Tommy, he's yanking and laughing; Samantha, she's with him, smirking; Sid Martin is pulling, frowning and grim; Sylvia, damn her, she's gleeful; even Andrea, and Twyla, and there's Glen—they all have a rope and a piece of me.

I come awake in a blink, my eyes open on full, staring straight up at the cottage-cheese ceiling. I'm wrapped up in the sheets, twisted from my battle with the ropes, and a ball-peen hammer is banging on my head from the inside. I kick the sheet off, massage my face, and go to the bathroom for an Excedrin. I plant my butt on the toilet seat, willing the drug to work *now*. I don't know how long I've been sitting when the Princess starts ringing. I stumble into the kitchen, my head still throbbing. It's Sid Martin. I squeeze my forehead with my free hand and look at the clock on the stove; it's only seven-thirty in the frigging a.m.

Martin is eager to meet and apologizes for not waiting for my call. There is a sense of panic in his voice as he nearly begs me to meet with him today. I put him off until tomorrow; I'll see him

140

at ten o'clock. The joy of my revenge is changing to the chagrin of witnessing another man's desperation.

After Sid Martin's call, I'm suddenly compelled to get ahold of Andrea. She's been more on my mind since my tête-à-tête with Sylvia. I tell her we need to talk about her dad before I go out to Vernonia again. What I don't say is that I just need to see her—that I want to see her.

I catch Andrea on her cell phone and she eagerly agrees to my invitation to dinner. It's a joy to hear another person's voice sparkle with the thought of being with you, just you (thank you, Sylvia). I suggest this Thai place over on Broadway. Andrea professes a fondness for Asian food; we'll meet at seven o'clock. That will give me time to see if I can reclaim my head and a reasonable thought process. I take a long, hot shower, then a nap, and yours truly regains his youth—well, after how I've felt, it seems that way.

Andrea is already at the Flower Bowl Thai restaurant when I walk in. She's smiling and waving at me from a table in a back corner. The place is busy. I walk by hunkered bodies, people totally absorbed in the plates in front of them, a few wrestling chopsticks. Andrea is rocking side to side in her chair, waiting for me with a welcoming smile the size of three fortune cookies. I can't match her smile, but I try, crinkling my out-of-practice cheek muscles. Then again, why am I weighing her smile on a scale of merit when she's looking only at me, her blue eyes interested only in me: paunchy, aimless, just coming back from vomiting in a planter box, me? I should be grateful; I am.

She is all breathy and toothy. "This table okay?"

I straddle the chair, lean on my elbows, and frown. "I usually sit by the front window."

"Oh, really? I'm sorry, bet we can…"

"Joke." I'm looking into her eyes and think that this is only the third time we've been together: coffee, sex, Thai. In that order.

"Oh, you." Her forbearing laugh excuses my juvenile humor. "It's nice to see you," she says, her voice quieting.

She looks good. She's wearing a men's style white button-down shirt, a blue blazer, and a discreet gold chain that dips below the hollow of her neck. And her hair looks less *done*, looser, more natural. I'm wearing the same khaki pants, and blue sport shirt, and my remaining hair is slicked back.

"And you," I say. "I like your hair."

She blushes and reaches up. "Oh. Thanks. I asked my hairdresser if it looked okay. You know, the way it was. She said no. Well, she really said no, unless I wanted to join the blue hair club."

"Ouch. Brutal."

"She got my attention."

A waitress cuts in. We order to share. Midway through too much food, Andrea raises the subject.

"So, you seeing Dad tomorrow?"

Then it dawns on me. I've agreed to meet with Sid Martin. "No, I have an appointment tomorrow."

"Really? I thought Tuesday is the only day you can see him."

"That's been working, hasn't it?"

"Well no, but..."

"You know what?" I say. "I'll just go out Wednesday. Why didn't I think of that before? Sure, Twyla will be gone, and just maybe I can catch Richard off guard."

Andrea looks worried. "But didn't she, this Twyla, say she needed to be around because of him being so sick?"

"That's what she said," I say. "She did say that. But, like they say, it's easier to ask for forgiveness than for permission. Right?"

"I guess so."

"Andrea, I will be very careful. I'm not going to hurt or endanger this man I love."

142

"What will you do if you get to see him?" she asks.

I shrug. "Talk. You know, get reacquainted. Have one of our backroom talks again. About life." She is looking at me, questioning. "Andrea, are you ready to go with me yet?"

She looks down at her pad Thai noodles and doesn't answer for a moment. "I don't know what it is," she says. "I...I want to. I need to, Edmund, I know that. I do. But when I think about it, I get the chills. Like I'm looking down from a very high place, that kind of chill. What am I going to do?"

"Let me give it one more try," I say. "I'll get him to see me. Then we'll have this wonderful reunion, the three of us. Okay?" I raise my bottle of Asian beer in a salute and take a swallow.

After a sigh she smiles. "Okay. A reunion—that will be nice."

"That it will," I say. "After that, we can get on with life. You up for that?"

She smiles shyly. "I think so."

"You better be."

"Your wife...ex-wife, have you seen her?" Her face crinkles around the eyes, ready to repel my answer. "Maybe I shouldn't ask."

"No, that's okay. Yes, I saw her." I laugh. "Actually, she came knocking at my door, believe it or not."

"Really? I can't imagine. If Cliff showed up at my door, I don't know what I'd do. How was that?"

"Weird," I say. "Not fun at all. But we finally aired out our feelings. Closure, I guess they call it. At least and at last we had it out. It's over, really over."

"So she doesn't fit into...your getting on with life?"

I shake my head and scoop some more broccoli and beef onto my plate. "No. My getting on with life has blue eyes in it...I think. What do you think?"

It takes a moment; then Andrea blushes and laughs. "Maybe," she says.

We smile our way through the rest of the meal and break open our fortune cookies. They have the same message: *First love is the sweetest.* We laugh so hard the waitress comes over to see if anything is wrong. I walk Andrea to her silver Lexus. We kiss gently, and I promise to let her know how my next attempt with Richard goes.

-18-

I pull into the old Singleton parking lot just after ten o'clock Tuesday morning. I am about to put what *was* up against what *is* and judge it against what *could be*—I'm not eager for the exercise. The place has a different paint scheme on the buildings, improved landscaping, and a huge new sign that declares this to be *Amalgamated-Durant Wholesale Foods*, and, in smaller lettering, *Singleton Division*. I walk unhurriedly to the main entrance, enter a fancy refurbished lobby, and immediately hear my name. The woman smiling at me from the receptionist's desk is Polly Page, a woman I had worked with for many years.

"Edmund," she says. "How nice to see you."

"Hi, Polly, good to see you, too. The place has really gone uptown."

"I guess it has." She smiles sheepishly. "Sorry, I'm supposed to let Mr. Martin know the minute you arrive." She punches the keypad of her phone; I hear her saying softly, "He's here". She smiles again and sits down at her desk as a stocky man approaches. He looks to be in his forties, has big teeth and a ruddy complexion.

"Edmund, Sid Martin. Good to see you," the man exudes, holding out a fleshy hand. "Come in, come in. Polly, bring coffee for three into my office, and ask Dan to join us."

I am ushered into what used to be Wernie Singleton's office. Business may be off, but the place has new furnishings: teak desk and tables, leather couch and cushy chairs. Dan Webb, a tall, athletic man, joins Sid Martin and me; he is maybe ten years younger than Martin. Polly Page enters carrying a tray with cups and a coffee urn. I wink, she; smiles, backs out, and closes the office door.

"Dan has your old job, Edmund," Sid Martin says. "We brought him in from our Omaha division." I just smile. "He worked with one of our top men back there, Red Richards. Have you heard of him, Edmund?"

"Sorry, no" I say.

"Red Richards is a legend," says Dan Webb. "Reinvented distribution technology."

"Yes, I understand that the tech side of things is fine, Dan," I say. "But I hear you are having customer relations problems. Can you fill me in on that?"

The young man flashes his irritation at my choice of words and pours himself some coffee. Before he can answer, Sid Martin breaks in.

"Well, like I told you on the phone, Edmund—"

"Excuse me, Sid," I say. "If you don't mind, I'd like to hear Dan's take on it. He's the person dealing with this matter directly. That okay?"

Sid Martin looks at his protégé. "Sure thing. Dan?"

Dan Webb stares at me for a long moment. "Okay," he says, "yeah, we have customer problems. But back in Omaha, we'd call it mollycoddling."

"I'm sorry," I respond.

"What I'm saying," Dan Webb says, "is that you Singleton people pampered your customers to such a degree that they expect to have their hands held over every little thing. With Red Richard's system, technology eliminates ninety percent of the costly one-on-one communication with customers, and everyone benefits."

"So, Dan," I say as calmly as I can, "I understand that you are losing customers. Is that right?" Dan Webb just stares at me. "Where are they going?"

"United Columbia Foods," answers Sid Martin. "Mostly."

I take a drink from my coffee cup. "Really? We used to take customers away from them. Say, do you still have the McCoy Markets as customers?"

"No, we lost them a month ago…to United Columbia," says Sid Martin.

"That so? I wooed them away from United ten years ago. Why did they leave?"

Dan Webb snorts. "Now, there's a good example. Sam McCoy must have called once a week with some ridiculous question that just wasted time and money."

"Sam's a great guy. They still have the four stores?" I ask.

"Yeah, four behind-the-times stores," Dan Webb says. "Old Sam still asks for you, if you think that matters."

"Customers should be asking for somebody," I say. "Personal touch counts."

"Look, maybe in your day, it did," Dan Webb says. "The hand-holding days are gone."

I look at Sid Martin. "Sorry, Sid. I don't think I'd fit in."

"Edmund, wait a minute. Let's talk this through. We're just frustrated is all," Sid Martin says. "We've been having a tough run of it here."

"I'm not your man," I say. "Dan here's your future, it seems like, if you can wait for him to catch on."

"Look, mister," Dan Webb almost stands up.

Sid Martin shakes his head. "Dan, hold on for minute, will you? So give me something, Edmund."

I look between the two men. "No, like Dan here's thinking, I'm yesterday's news. I just hope your technology can catch up while you're twisting in the wind."

147

As I'm on the way out, Polly Page looks up from her desk and smiles hopefully. I shake my head. Her smile fades. I raise my hand; she waves back. I push through the door and feel a thickening in my throat. What the hell—why do I have to close doors twice? Sylvia comes knocking, dangles a revival that neither of us wants, and then rejects me all over again. Now the ghost of Singleton toys with me, begging for an encore, but I can't carry that tune anymore.

Now I have to go find my future—the real one. I wonder what it is?

-19-

It is Wednesday, not Tuesday, and I'm firing up the Chevelle at seven thirty-eight. Just over Sylvan Hill on 26 it starts to rain. By the North Plains off-ramp it's pouring, and I'm driving through a thrashing waterfall. The used-up old wiper blades are smearing on the down swipe and missing everything on the up. I creep into Manning, squinting and braking at every shadow. A note is taped to the door at Jerry's garage: *Back in 10 minutes.* I leave instructions scribbled on the back of a grocery receipt, stick it under a wiper blade, and sprint for the nursery.

Glen grants me entrance to the trailer and tosses me a stringy towel. She watches me blot and wipe, still wearing her pajamas and a shapeless brown bathrobe. Her hair is down, hanging at shoulder length. It makes her seem less tough. By the time I dry and comb my hair, she is holding out a cup of coffee. Up to this point we haven't said more than six words between us. I sniff; the place smells musty.

"Damn flash flood out there," I say.

"Spring. What you doing out this early? Not coming to work, are ya?" She wrinkles her face.

"No. Heading to Vernonia. Got caught in the downpour with wipers fanning nothing but air. Left the car at Jerry's for new blades."

Glen runs her fingers through her hair. "Thought you only went out there on Tuesdays."

"'I usually do. Decided to try a different approach."

"Breakfast? Eggs? Toast? Got Wheaties."

"Nah, this is fine. Just in out of the rain until the garage opens."

She nods, leans a hip against the counter, folds her arms, and stares at me.

"What? Something hanging out of my nose?" I swipe at my nostrils.

She shakes her head. "Just thinking."

"Too damned early for that," I say. "Like what? You thinking what?"

"About happenstance. Not a believer in coincidence," she says. "Things don't just happen, leastwise not to my way of thinking. There's a reason for everything."

"What the heck are you talking about? What things? This your morning muse?" I grin.

She pours more coffee. I stretch my legs out from where I'm sitting on the built-in couch and suck hot liquid over the lip of the cup and stare back at her. She pulls a pack of cigarettes and a Bic lighter out of the patch pocket on her robe and lights up: Camels, no filter.

"Okay, so you're thinking I'm no accidental tourist," I say.

She exhales, her smile faint, and says, "My mother died when I was three." I raise my eyebrows; she keeps on. "In less'n a year my father remarried. Heloise. Heloise had a daughter, older'n me by fifteen years." She sucks on the cigarette, her cheeks collapsing. "Daughter's name was Twyla. Twyla Ann."

I lower my cup and wait for her to go on.

"Not a real common name, Twyla. Now is it?"

"Glen, what's…the woman up the road?" I hook a thumb up. "You shittin' me?"

150

Glen is shaking her head and tapping ashes. "Nope."

"Jesus, this is too weird. How'd you know...when I was drunk? I say something? Use her name?"

"Bourbon, the great truth serum."

"This Twyla," I ask, "is the same one living with my guy? You're sure...the same person? Is that what you're saying?"

"Yep, Heloise's daughter is one and the same." Glen is standing in a cloud of smoke. Our eyes are locked.

"You're sure?" I repeat.

She nods. "That night, when you said her name, I knew she was tangled up in your thing? Gave me the crawlies."

"Life happens."

"No, it don't," she says. "Like why are you here on a Wednesday? In a gully washer. On your way out there. And lookie there," she points out the window, "sun's out, ain't rainin'. You don't even need new wipers now. But here you are." She draws on the cigarette hard again. "Now...now I gotta tell you."

This tough broad is shaking when I stand in front of her, put my cup down on the counter, and hold her by her shoulders. "What is it, Glen?"

"We were never close, me and her," she says, sounding almost apologetic. "Not like real sisters. She left home when I was still in grade school. And she's not my blood anyway."

"Glen, what?"

She slumps back against the counter. "She comes by every couple of months. Twyla. You know, howdy, howdy, have a drink."

"Damn it, Glen. Tell me."

She puts a hand over her mouth and closes her eyes for a moment then takes in a deep breath. "Okay. A while back she tells me about this old guy she's living with."

"Richard Vickerman?" The chill I'm getting is not good.

"She used the name Richard, yes."

151

"Go on."

"Anyway, she gloats about getting the fella to move in with her, said she's got some financial security for a change. Told me he's real sick but has some money put away, and she's thinking he'll leave her fixed and that he ain't got long."

"He's got a daughter," I say. "He wouldn't do that."

Glen sniffs. "I don't know, what I'm thinking is she's...she's maybe abusing the old guy. Something she said. Something like: *I get tough with him if I have to.* Handles all his money, too."

"This can't be." The pit of my stomach is cramping. "Damn!"

"Twyla, she isn't part of me." Glen's eyes are wet. "She's a mean one. My old man would knock her around. Then she'd beat on me. Bad times."

When I hug her, the wiry rawboned toughness has melted back some. The nursery yard is fogging with heated wetness when I charge through it. I stuff money in Jerry's hand, thank him, and give the Chevelle its head. On the moist, steaming asphalt, I slither more than once when hitting a curve too hard. But I stay on the road, my mind swirling with anger and fear. All is calm when I turn onto Mississippi; the only person outside is a woman bent over weeding a lost-cause flowerbed, her blue housedress hiked up, revealing white, fleshy legs. The Honda isn't parked in the driveway, just the Pinto on soft tires. I let the car idle for a moment before killing the ignition; my heart is pounding.

What am I going to do—charge inside and drag Richard to safety? I sit hunched forward with my hands draped over the steering wheel and watch the house as if it might explode in front of me. After a couple of minutes I go to the door. There is no answer to my knock. I try the doorknob; it's locked. I knock again, nothing. I find him around in back of the house. He's sitting in a weathered Adirondack chair, wearing the fedora, his eyes closed and head back with the sun on his face. When I touch his shoulder, his eyes open slowly, and he looks up into my face, studying. He smiles with thin pasty lips.

"Edmund," he says, "you've come."

I squat down. "I'm sorry, Richard, I didn't know."

"Oh?" he says in a soft, whispery voice. "And what didn't you know?"

"About Twyla."

He tips his head back again and closes his eyes. The sun mocks his paleness. "Twyla, you've met her, I know," he says. "She told me so."

"What did she tell you about me?"

He smiles and opens those eyes I know from the past. "That you believed her story. But you kept coming back anyway. You're a stubborn one, she says."

"You told me to go away, though," I say.

"Did I?" His smile fades. "Yes, I thought it best. But here you are again. Twyla will be upset. Guests on Tuesdays only. The rule."

"Richard," I say, "are you all right?"

"Right now, here in the spring sun, I'm feeling tolerable. Best I can do, though, because my lungs are killing me."

"No, I mean are you being hurt...abused?"

He raises an arm and rolls up the sleeve of his shirt. The frailty and the slack skin stun me, but it is the nest of bruises on his forearm that makes me flinch and bite down.

"My god, what happened?"

"I understand that I fall a lot," he says.

"Is she doing this?"

"I read your notes, Edmund," he says, ignoring my question. "Twyla let me have them. I have been thinking back on the old days. We did have some good times at old Bob-Buys, didn't we?"

"Richard," I square around so I can see his face, "Richard, why don't you just leave? Get away from her, call someone for help—like your daughter, Andrea."

After a moment of thought, he says, "Haven't seen her in some time. We don't talk anymore." He coughs. "Do you remember Andrea?"

I hesitate. "Sure, I remember her. I had a crush on her back when you and I were at Gilson's and she would come in."

"Sit down, Edmund, please. There pull that…see that old chair? Pull that over here. That's the one. There now. Sit."

I do as he says and sit on the slack-jointed kitchen chair. "Richard," I begin again, "this can't go on."

He doffs the stained felt hat and sets it in his lap. His white hair is thin, and the wisps flit about in the short breeze. "Sun feels good, doesn't it? Rained like sic 'em less than an hour ago." He pauses and inhales deeply, his chest rising. He sees me watching him catch his breath. "I must look something awful to you."

"You look fine," I lie.

"Dang Chesterfields. God, I loved 'em—two packs a day, sometimes three. Might say I loved them to death, Edmund, 'cause they're killing me now. Sick lungs. Not a thing to wish on your worst enemy. No sir. Gradually cutting off my air. You've heard of the emphysema?"

"Yes," I say. "Let me get you out of here. Get you to a specialist."

"Done that already. Too late, nothing to be done except sit in the sun when I can and think on better times. Like we had. Like that," he says. "We had some good times, didn't we?"

"That's why I'm here, why I've been coming. I want to see Dick Vic again. To touch base with the one man whom I admire above all others."

He inhales a ragged breath and leans forward, elbows on his knees. "My, my, and why are you wanting to do that? You've been very persistent, I must say. Something troubling you?"

I look down, scoot a clod of dirt around with my toe, and now I can't think of a thing to say. I can hear Richard's breathing; it's a horrible sound. What did Felix say? Find it, look it in the face, decide, and move on. I look into Richard's tired, yellowed eyes, lean on my knees like he is, and chuckle.

"Yeah, something's troubling me," I say. "My life, that's what. Been in the dumper for a spell."

He turns his head toward me. "Is that so?"

He begins to cough and cough and spits a glob of something into a foul handkerchief. He sits back, breathing horribly, and apologizes for being obscene to watch.

"Wretched to look on another person rotting away right in front of you."

I sit quietly and wait and feel the heat of tears behind my eyes. Richard sits still and breathes and stares off across the scruffy backyard.

"Can't imagine you in the dumper, Edmund," he says when he can. He turns his eyes back on me. His chest rises. "Not the Edmund I knew."

The chair groans and sways when I sit up and plant my hands on my thighs. "You remember those long talks we used to have in the back room at Gilson's and then in your office at Bob-Buys? Remember those times?"

"I do, I surely do." He leans his head back and closes his eyes again. "My, that was so long ago.

I laugh. "Then you must remember that I was in the dumper a lot when I was young and floundering through life. And you listened to my young-man pain and anguish. Those huge problems seem so ridiculous now. But at the time I needed someone to listen and treat my crises as real—that person was you."

Richard's chest rises and falls as I talk; he struggles to breathe.

"You know, Edmund," he says, "usually about the time a boy's growing crotch hair and a few whiskers there's at least one grown-up male around who seems bigger than he really is to the kid. Happens to most of us. Guys like that, they seem to stand taller and to understand our pining better than anyone else. Sure as hell better than our own folks—at least we think so."

A slide show blinks on in my head. I think of my dad in Phoenix. I think of his pain because I'd chosen Richard to hear my questions and help me solve my boyish dilemmas. I feel regret so deeply for those years my father endured his sadness over my choice. Regret is an awful punishment, especially when it comes too late.

"But our heroes," Richard continues and raises a long-nailed forefinger, "they end up being as flawed as everyone else. I sure was." He pauses and breathes slowly. After a minute he says, "Now then, why are you here?"

"I owe you," I answer. He smiles into the sun, eyes closed, and shakes his head. "Don't be shaking your head, now," I say. You gave the young man I used to be a head start. I needed to tell you that."

"What else?" he asks. "That's not really why you're here."

"I want you to listen—like you used to."

He smiles. "You finally figured it out. I had no answers, just ears—that's all it was." He inhales slowly. "There goes your all-wise sage, huh?"

"Richard," I admonish mildly, "I'm here to rewind."

"You can do that?"

"We'll see."

"So what happened?"

"Oh, for starters, divorce. Sylvia's gone." Richard's eyes open on me. "That's right," I confirm.

"I always liked Sylvia," he says. "Of course, I only knew the face she showed me."

"Me too," I say, trying to smile. "Then again, she only knew the face I showed her, too."

Richard breathes in deep and waits. "Guess we all do that," he says finally, "show different faces."

"Yeah."

"What else?" he asks.

"Wernie Singleton sold out," I say.

Richard stares straight ahead at that. "Wernie sold out? To who?"

"Outfit from Ohio, Amalgamated-Durant."

"Never heard of 'em. Let me guess: they dumped you."

"Yeah, in the dumper," I joke.

"Their loss," he says ignoring my humor.

"Funny thing is, they called and wanted me back. I went to see them but walked away."

"That so? Why's that?"

I thought for a moment. "Same thing," I answer. "We were showing different faces. It didn't feel right."

"Uh-huh." Richard sighs as the sun plays on his face. "You got the double whammy, didn't you? Now what?"

"I'm working on it," I say

We sit in the sun, quiet, and the breeze pushes past us, each sitting with his own thoughts. We are quiet like that for a spell before we hear the pop and crunch of tires on gravel and a car door slamming. Twyla's back.

-20-

Richard's body becomes even more rigid, and the little piece of serenity bleeds out of his face with Twyla on the grounds. It doesn't take her long to find us. We hear her tramping through the house calling out, opening and slamming doors. Neither of us speaks as we wait. I hear the back door open, but I don't turn to look. She must be studying us first, because it is several moments before the spring on the screen door complains. It's as if someone is standing behind me with a loaded weapon; I want to duck. Richard has his head back and his eyes closed, and I am looking down at my feet when she walks up.

"Well, well," she says, "Edmund."

I raise my head and smile; guess it's more of a grimace. "Twyla."

Her bulbous nose and her cheeks are aflame, and her eyes are darting. "Missed you yesterday."

"Something came up. But here we are, anyway, finally connected. Richard and me."

"So I see," she says, her voice brittle.

"Must have been the Tuesday thing," I say. "We were outta sync on Tuesdays. You think, maybe?"

"No," she says, hands on her hips, "no, I don't think maybe."

"Sure, must be," I say. "Has to be. We've been having a great time catching up on the old days and all."

"No never mind," she says, "that this man is sick, sicker than you know. I don't allow people to come 'round unless I'm here. For his own good. I don't appreciate you just showing up like this."

"That right? I don't agree." I reach out and touch Richard's arm. "We've been sitting here quiet, talking, taking in the sun. Getting along fine as frog's hair."

"Really? Well tell me now, Edmund," Twyla says, "would you know what to do if he had one of his spells? Having people show up unannounced gets him stirred up. Can send him off on one of them coughing jags of his. Know what cupping is? Here, Richard, lean over." She goes behind him and shoves shoulders forward until he's propped onto his elbows. He begins to cough; and, when he does, she starts pounding on his back with her hands, hard, hard blows. His pathetic torso bounces with each strike. She administers one blow after another, and I swear her face is a mask of anger. This is not therapy; this is punishment.

"Wait." I jump up and grab one of her wrists. "Stop, you're hurting him."

Twyla steps back and grins. "See what I mean? That's cupping." She holds out her hands, fingers curled into a curved palm. "The man's lungs are full of phlegm. Only way to get any of it out is to mobilize it so he can cough it up. We get two to three full cups of yellow crud out every day. Every dad-blamed day. And you can't do it by rubbing his back nicey-nice. You gotta beat it out of him. This ain't for sissies."

"From where I was sitting it looked like you were relishing the walloping too much." I lay a hand on Richard's shoulder, and it rides up and down with each labored breath. I pat him gently.

"What do you know about it? Flitting in and out of here looking for the nostalgia of the old days. Stirring things up like it

159

makes a difference. We've got a life to save here, mister. You don't have a clue what it takes day after day. Up in the night, medication, cleaning up after him, cooking for him…"

"All right." I raise a hand. "Enough. I know enough."

She glares; the affable person I'd seen before is no longer. "Think so? You don't know a damn thing. You know nothing."

I look into her eyes; they shine with anger made all the more menacing by her hard, acne-scarred face. "Oh, I know things," I say and instantly feel Richard's body move beneath my hand. He's looking up, shaking me off ever so slightly. But he doesn't understand where I'm going.

Twyla stiffens with my claim and folds her arms across her bosom. "Really? What things?"

Richard is still looking at me; he starts to cough, an obvious diversionary tactic. I keep my hand on his shoulder and move it reassuringly. "Oh, for instance, I know your sister."

I can honestly say that I'd never seen the blood drain from a person's face; I thought it was a myth until this moment. Twyla's florid face is transformed from inflamed to ashen in a speechless moment while she stands transfixed, digesting what I've said. When it appears that the full impact has hit bottom, she turns around once and faces me again with this twisted smile.

"Be damned," she says. "Glenda Bee. That's what I always called her when we was kids. So Glenda. You know Glenda?" I nod. "The plant lady who loves her bourbon. Small world."

"Funny," I say. "Glen said pretty much the same thing this morning when I stopped by the nursery. Something about happenstance."

Twyla glances down at Richard's upturned face. "We're not close. Fact is…yeah, Richard, just came to me that I never told you about my little sis. Well, we aren't blood, not even half sisters. Sisters by divorce. We're what, guess maybe thirteen years apart?"

"Fifteen," I say.

She shrugs. "Something like that. How you know Glenda?"

"I work for her. Part-time, help out around the yard and with customers."

"That right? Didn't think she did enough business to feed herself, let alone have a hired hand. Big career move for you, was it?"

"I like it."

"I'll just bet," she says, smirking.

"Funny how this is all connected up—you, Glen, Richard, me," I say.

She sets her jaw. "Come on, Richard. Need to get you inside for lunch and your meds then a nap. I've got two more houses to clean this afternoon."

I hold Richard down with my hand. "Wait. Won't take a minute to finish the story about Glen." Twyla steps toward Richard. I move between them. "The story is your story, Twyla Ann, the one you told Glen last time you stopped by. A real-rags-to-riches story, about financial security and all. About your windfall, wasn't it?"

The flame reappears in Twyla's face; her rage is spiked with a tinge of fear. I am relishing the unveiling, but Richard wrestles himself up out of the yard chair and stands wheezing and shaking his head.

"No, Edmund," he says, struggling the words out. "Leave us be now." We wait between short sentences. "I know you care, but this kind of thing...will...no, you got to leave us to ourselves now." When I open my mouth to protest, he takes hold of my arm. "Please."

I step back, clamp my mouth shut, and shake my head at him. It is his turn to pat me as he shuffles by and allows Twyla to hold his arm and help him into the house. I stand in the yard angry and afraid for Dick Vic. I'm in the same spot when Twyla comes back out, letting the screen door slam, and stomps across to me. She's breathing hard.

"Listen, you," she says, "get off this property now, and don't ever come back. I'll call the cops on you if you do."

"You won't call the cops now or any time, and we both know it," I threaten.

Her eyes widen. "Like hell I won't."

"Okay, call them. Right now. Yeah, right now. Then we'll all talk about elder abuse, theft, manipulation of assets, maybe fraud. Hell, I don't know that's just for starters."

Her mouth opens and closes, but nothing comes out.

"I'll bring Glen in as a witness. Oh, don't like that one bit, do you? So for right now, Richard seems to want me out of this. That's short term. And let me warn you, Twyla—look at me—let me warn you, Richard isn't going to fall down anymore. Nada, nyet, no more." I stop to catch my breath from hyperventilating. "Because I promise you, any physical harm you do to him I'll do twice to you."

"You can't threaten me like that." Her face is aflame.

"Not a threat," I say. "You know the cliché—it's a promise. Besides, this is between you and me. I'll be back. In the meantime, you'd better be sure his property remains his property, his money remains his money, and his health doesn't suddenly deteriorate. Now move that damn Honda outta my way."

-21-

In Manning, I slow and start to turn in at the nursery but don't and feel guilty about it all the way home. My head is full of thoughts of Glen morose and drinking. I start to take an off-ramp and go back; but, what the hell, she'd drink through it anyway. At the apartment, I park the Chevelle in the lot and have already decided what I have to do next: call Andrea. We need to get Richard out of there. I cut across the apartment grounds and stride past Felix sitting on our bench, smoking. He stares at me as I rush by. I hesitate, start to explain myself, but to hell with that. Besides, Felix is only an observer, not a critic; a person has to care about something to get steamed.

Andrea answers her cell phone on the first ring.

"Edmund," she says, all warmlike, "I was just thinking—"

"I saw Richard this morning," I interrupt.

"Really? You really saw my dad? Edmund!"

"Wait, before that, I stopped at this nursery I work at part time."

"Nursery, what nursery?" Andrea asks, perplexed.

"A place in Manning, you know, that little burg on the way to the coast…forget that, I'll tell you later. Anyway, the owner, woman named Glen…Glenda is the owner." I take a deep breath to level out my heartbeat. "You're not going to believe this, but

163

that Twyla woman, the one living with Richard, is Glen's adopted sister."

"What? I don't understand."

"Never mind. Andrea, get over here right away. To my apartment."

"Edmund, I can't. I'm right in the middle—"

"Forget whatever you're doing!" I'm almost shouting. "Your dad is in danger."

"I don't understand," she says, her voice rising. "In what kind of danger? Tell me!"

"Glen thinks her sister is abusing your dad. After confronting Twyla this morning, I'm convinced Glen's right. Now I need you. I don't trust that bitch. We have to get your dad the hell away from there. I came back for you to keep things legal."

"My god," Andrea gasps. "I…I'm coming, right now." Her phone clicks off.

Andrea plows into the parking lot fifteen minutes later. I reject a ride in her Lexus, and we charge off in the Chevelle; she grabs on to the armrest of the beast and hangs on. I cut over to the Fremont Bridge and emerge from the Vista Ridge tunnel onto 26, hit the outside lane, and let the Chevelle air out a chunk of its 350 horses. Andrea sits still and looks straight ahead. We're passing everything. I idle down in Manning and consider pulling off at the nursery but don't. I'll explain it all to Andrea later.

At the Vernonia turnoff, I spot the blue Honda sitting at the Texaco station pumps and point it out to Andrea. Twyla's gassing up; the car is facing east and away from Vernonia. She's running a squeegee over the windshield; her back is to us. No one is in the car. Andrea looks over her shoulder as we pass. She keeps watching until we've driven out of sight then reaches out and places a hand on my thigh. When I look over, she is staring out the side window. I put my hand on top of hers and press the accelerator down; the Chevelle groans its pleasure. We thunder beneath the trestles.

I drive slowly down Bridge Street and ignore shouts from two teenage boys who are giving the car thumbs-up. Andrea and I haven't spoken since leaving Portland; we know what we're up to. When the house comes into view, my body is raging with its built-in alarms. Andrea paws at the door handle the instant we roll to a stop. I grab her arm and lie to her that I want to prepare Richard for seeing his estranged daughter. She looks at me, and her eyes darken, rejecting any thought of staying behind. She pulls away and scoots out of the car.

Richard is sitting in the battered recliner. An oxygen tank stands behind the chair; an elastic band is holding a cannula to his nose; the cannula is attached to a plastic line running from the tank. He is watching television when we come in, a fishing program. He had always loved to fly fish. I walk up and grip his shoulder; he nods, reaches up, and pats the back of my hand, and continues to watch the program.

"I've come to get you, Richard," I say. "Both of us have. Me and Andrea."

With the mention of his daughter's name, he stiffens but doesn't turn his head or otherwise react to the presence of his child. "I know," he says. "She told me you would be coming."

"Are you all right?" I step in front of him; Andrea stays back massaging her hands.

His left eye is swollen shut, the eyelid crimson, and his right cheekbone is puffed up and blue-black. There is a laceration across the wound, and a line of coagulated red sags down. I groan and lean over. "Damn it."

"What?" Andrea comes up, and for the first time in a long time, looks into the face of her father. She cringes and inhales. "Daddy, oh my god."

"Going away present." He tries to laugh and starts to cough

and can't stop until he has hacked four or five times; by that time, his chest is heaving. He leans forward, elbows on the recliner arms, and wheezes in and out. In between breaths he says *water*. Andrea rushes off. Richard and I listen to the clatter of finding a glass, the hiss of the faucet, and the hard-heeled tapping of her return. Richard takes several small swallows and leans back in the chair. "Turn off that dang television," he says. "Won't ever cast another line again."

"When we get things set right, I'll take you fly fishing," I say. "Count on it."

He smiles and closes his eyes. "Maybe I could watch you. Would be nice to be on a river again. Maybe we could go to the Metolius. I love that river."

"Sure. We'll go to Camp Sherman, rent us a cabin." I smile at Andrea. Her face is anesthetized, her eyes locked on me, wide, unblinking.

I shut off the television.

"Richard," I say and kneel down and wait until he opens his eyes. "Andrea's here."

He frowns. "Heard you the first time."

"She's been worried about you. You know, all this time." When he says nothing, I say, "She helped me find you."

"She's got no use for me. Not after her mother...not after that."

Andrea is standing back, unsure. She advances to where she can see him again, closes her eyes at his appearance, bolsters herself, and raises her eyelids. "Daddy, it's okay now. Isn't it?" Her voice comes out higher, childlike.

Richard doesn't meet her eyes. He coughs and tries to clear his throat. I hand him the water glass again. He gulps twice, hands the glass back. "I gotta pee," he says.

He leans forward, wrestles the recliner upright, then pushes up out of the chair and stands, wavering. When I reach out he says, "Leave me be. I can do it."

He pulls the cannula off, and we watch him totter down the hall and hear the door shut behind him.

"Andrea, it'll be all right. Give him some time." I reach out and touch her shoulder, she leans her head against my chest, and we wait. I point out the thunder eggs; she smiles and picks one up and rolls it around in her hand. And we wait. Too long.

When I finally go to the bathroom door and knock and call his name, he is already gone. By the time I overcome good manners and enter the bathroom, Richard has a lead on us. The door we heard closing was the back door. I stomp from room to room, cursing, before bursting out the back door and looking around. Richard is nowhere.

When I go back inside, Andrea is still in shock trying to imagine that her father lives in this place. It takes her a moment to realize what I'm saying: that Dick Vic has skipped out and that we have to find a sick old man in a hurry. He can't be far. We quickly decide that I will search the neighborhood on foot and Andrea will drive my car over the nearby streets and honk if she sees him. I crash out the back again, slamming the screen door open, make a directional decision, and strike off across back yards. My heart is pounding out my fear and my stupidity. In the background the Chevelle rumbles to life, and I can only hope it's not too much car for Andrea. I crisscross the yards, bang on doors, rousing startled neighbors. No one has seen Richard, but all promise to keep an eye out for him.

Okay, we've searched. He's gone. Damn it to hell! We are sitting in his house amongst his rocks, exhausted and anxious. One old man who can't breathe enough to keep a guppy alive and who is so weak he can hardly stand has vanished. At least he has evaded these two disoriented searchers. I call the Vernonia Police Department; they take down the details and promise to have their people keep an eye out and call if they locate Richard. Of course, they can't list him as a missing person after his being gone for only little more than an hour. "But he's terribly sick," I tell them. The officer I talk with says not to worry. It's a small town; someone's sure to spot him.

The hours drag; the phone doesn't ring. I go out looking again, first on foot and then in the Chevelle. Nothing. Shadows are getting deep by the time I get back from this last trip around the back streets and down through town, again with nothing to show for it. Andrea meets me out on the porch. The police haven't called. I hold her, she holds me, and we stand like that for a long time. What else can we do? I keep going back out and tramping the streets. It's near dusk, and I'm returning from one more search when a neighbor lady comes out and waves me down. Hers was the first door I'd banged on when Richard went missing.

"Have you found him yet?" she asks.

"No, and I've been over the town at least three times," I say.

The woman is maybe in her fifties, graying brown hair. "No luck at all?" she says, her face crimped in an expression of deep concern.

"None," I answer. "And I'm getting concerned about him maybe being out all night. He's very sick."

"Yes, I know," she says. She turns and looks back toward her house. A man has come out on the porch and is watching us.

The woman chews on a knuckle and offers me a weak smile. "That's my husband," she says. "We sort of watch out for Richard."

"Watch out for him?"

She hesitates. "Well…I may be talking out of school, but this seems serious."

"What is it?"

"When you came to our door?"

"Yes?"

"Richard was there, in our house." When my eyebrows go up, she says, "You see, he asked me to let him wait there for a bit. Said there were some people at his house that he didn't want to see."

"One is his own daughter," I say, "who's been looking for him."

"It's just that…well, she is sometimes hard on him. There's yelling and such."

"She? You mean Twyla?"

"Yes." The woman gives me a worrisome smile. "I'm sorry. I thought I was doing the right thing."

"Is he still with you?"

"No, he left quite a while ago. My husband and I don't know where he is. I'm so sorry. I promise we'll let you know if we see him."

I thank the woman and go back to the house. There's been no call from the police. Andrea and I try to sleep but can only doze fitfully. I get up several times, go outside and stand on the porch, as if my peering into the dark will make Richard materialize. Nothing. Around first light, Andrea gets up to use the bathroom then rummages around in the kitchen and manages to brew some coffee. When the pounding comes on the front door, we're sitting side by side on the couch over steaming cups, staring at the floor. I look at my watch; it's six o'clock. We have been going over what to do next: call the police for the umpteenth time or start searching again. The man at the door is thick-bodied, with short black hair, wearing a white tee shirt, blue jeans, and boots. One hand is jammed in a back pocket; the other is working a toothpick in his open mouth. He looks familiar, then it comes to me that I saw him when I was first out looking for Richard. He lives about three houses over.

"You found the old man yet?" he asks.

"No. No, we haven't." I rub a knuckle in one eye.

"Damn," he says and ducks his head and looks away.

"Why, you seen him?"

"Not me, but I was just down to the café having breakfast. Think one of the boys down there saw him."

Then Andrea's there, her shoulder touching mine. "Did they find him? Dad, you found him?" Her voice is hyped up.

The fellow nods to Andrea. "Like I say, was having breakfast and—"

"Got that," I cut in, "where did he see him?"

"Okay," the man straightens up. "Well, this fella says it was last night after dark. Buster, guy who saw him, said it was out by the cemetery, the old one, Pioneer Cemetery."

"Damn, that means he's been outside all night," I say. "Okay, how do you get to the cemetery from here?"

The guy stops probing with this toothpick and eyes me. "Fella, you look the worse for it. What say you let me run you out there?"

It's an argument, but Andrea agrees to stay behind in case the police call on the landline; the battery on her cell phone is dead. We cling to each other before I clamber into the guy's mustard yellow Suburban. From the porch, Andrea frowns and chews on a fingernail as we back away. Our eyes are locked on one another until the guy in the tee shirt cramps the wheel, and we're gone. All the way down the hill into town he's rehashing how this guy Buster saw an old man but thought nothing of it until later. While he is grunting of rotten luck, I'm thinking of Richard being out overnight, the damp chill covering him like a suffocating blanket. I shudder and hate myself because it works to do so; that's my appeasement. In the center of town, the guy turns off Bridge Avenue onto State, and we lumber along under speed to where the street curves left and turns into Keasey Road. Houses become less frequent, and more trees border the road. Suddenly he wheels the Suburban off the road onto a gravel parking lot notched in next to a grove of huge evergreens and noses the rig right up against a chain-link fence. Timeworn monuments stand in contrast to the green patch of ground like teachers in the hallway, severe sentinels.

The guy leaves the engine running, drapes his arms over the steering wheel, and swivels his head about. We stare in nervous silence in a dreadful game of *I Spy*.

"Don't see nobody." He breaks the silence. "You?"

"Nope." Just the markers staring at us. "Better look."

The guy shuts off the engine, and we exit the Suburban. I kick through a klatch of empty beer cans and send them scattering. The guy growls, "Damn kids," and pushes the double chain-link gate open. We start looking row by row.

-22-

We find Richard leaning up against the backside of a big granite marker that's standing in for Margaret P. Smythe, 1859–1926 and Pope L. Smythe, 1844–1926. At least they went together. Richard's eyes are clamped shut, the maimed one clotted with matter; his arms are lifeless beside him, his body that of a raggedy doll propped against the cold stone. The guy in the tee shirt grunts when he sees him. I rush over, drop to my knees, and lift Richard's limp left arm. I press the wrist between my thumb and fingers then lean my head against his chest. I feel a weak pulse and can hear a heartbeat.

"He's alive," I say to the Suburban guy.

The man comes over and looks over my shoulder at Richard. "Damn, he musta taken a header in the dark. Look at his face. Jesus."

I lean up close to Richard and touch his face with my fingertips. "Richard." My voice falters; I clear my throat and say his name again, louder, and gently shake his shoulder. His eyes open as if he is coming out of a dream, and maybe he is. His good eye and mine meet when I face him. I say his name again, and he lowers his good eyelid.

"Can you talk?" I ask and notice then how damp his shirt is from the dew and slip out of my jacket and drape it over him.

When he answers, his voice is but a whisper. "What, Richard?" I ask. "I didn't catch it."

"I said, have you decided?" He opens the only lid that works and looks straight into my eyes. The raw bruise on his cheekbone glares at me.

I pat Richard, stand up, and face the guy standing behind me. "Do you have a cell phone?"

Guy nods. "In my rig."

"There an ambulance?"

"At the fire station. I'll get on it," he says wagging a forefinger and trotting off.

I sit down beside Richard, lean against the cold granite, and take his left hand in my right; his skin feels like rice paper. From a few steps away, it would seem that he is merely an elderly man resting comfortably in the sun, which has broken out now and is sweating the nighttime moisture out of the ground. All seems as it is not. A rattling wheeze gives testimony to Richard's desperate phase.

The guy comes trotting back; the ambulance is on its way. I ask him if he'll go get Andrea and bring her back here. He stares at the sack of meal that is Richard for a moment then says, "Sure thing," and trots off again. I squeeze Richard's hand.

"Everything will be all right, Richard." My voice has the sound of triteness and untruth, but I say the words anyway.

He gurgles and coughs. "No, Edmund. But it will be over."

"That's right. The ambulance will be here soon." I say. "Fix you up."

He moves his head from side to side in a denial he is too weary to waste his breath on.

I squeeze his hand; the bones are brittle reeds. "You'll be fine."

"Never be fine. Don't want to be fine."

I have no response for that, so I just watch him breathe.

Minutes are slipping by. I jump when he speaks again, leaning toward him, ready to offer help I cannot give him.

"What?" I say.

He coughs, inhales slowly, and says, "Why did you come? Really."

"Like I said, to see Dick Vic again. Get my life in order." I laugh, but it's not a real laugh. "You were a rock for me back then. You know that." I pat his hand again.

He starts to laugh, but that convulses into a coughing fit. I watch until he stops and spits off to the side away from me. He takes several even breaths then says, "A rock. That's rich. Pee gravel maybe." He pauses to breathe. He turns the good eye more directly on me, and we laugh. He rests, his breathing audible.

"So, why'd you run off like that?' I ask. "Andrea has been terrified for you."

His chest rises and falls, lungs captured in a rigid vest of rib bones. "Andrea," he says. "She never understood. She watched the battle and hated me for it."

"Her mother's cancer?"

He nods and wheezes. "That was the easy part—the battle. How could she understand the hard part?"

Holding my tongue is not easy, but I'm waiting for him to go on. The sun plays across our shirts and faces, and my line of vision is zeroed in on a fence post with a small black bird that is dancing around on it. I stay shut, say nothing.

"My brave Dottie." Richard pulls his hand out of mine and places it in his lap over his other hand. "She wanted the fight. God, she was tough. She coerced me with her courage and her love of me. How could I deny her? I couldn't." He sucks in another tortured breath and waits for the energy to go on. "It was our private hell. We couldn't include Andrea or the others in what we planned…we just couldn't."

"Why? Andrea would have understood," I say. "I'm sure of it."

"We had to protect her." He pauses and levels his breathing, then through pursed lips: "At least we thought we did. Maybe we were wrong…keeping Andrea away." He takes a breath. "I don't know."

"I'm sorry that it didn't work," I say.

"But it did," he says. "And that's why I went away yesterday. You see…and now, Edmund, here's *my* confession. Dottie didn't die on her own. It was me—I ended her struggle, took her life. No way would Andrea have accepted that then…maybe even now. What we did. Dottie and me. We agreed to fight it. But if the poisons weren't enough, we had our pact." He stares off and inhales; it is a strangling aspiration. "Got 'em to let me take her home." He quit talking right then for a bit, sat quiet like he was rewinding videotape.

"I remember her kiss. And her smile. And the way she looked at me. We held each other…and said goodbye." He raises a hand to his mouth, and his bony body shakes in private grief.

What can I say? What do you do when you hear such things, the pain and the horror of it? I sit very still, barely breathe, and hope it is not true but know it is. He suddenly leans forward and sniffs.

"Then." He pauses. "Then…I put the pillow over her face." He extends his arms, fingers spread, palms down. "She is smiling and doesn't resist." He lowers his arms, pressing down in midair. "I don't know how long it was before I knew she was gone. I just did. Then I lifted her head and put the pillow behind her, kissed her one more time, smelled her hair, straightened her bedclothes, and called her doctor." He sags back again. "We buried her and I shouldered my daughter's wrath and we went away, Dottie and me—with our secret. She's never left me."

"Richard," I say, "Andrea should hear this. She loves you, I know. It will be different now. It will."

He turns to me. "You tell her, Edmund." His breath is sour. "I can't. Dottie and me, we knew what we were doing, but still the one left behind can never be free of guilt. You can't know the pain from that kind of strangling guilt. I did for Dottie, but I can't ask Andrea to share that with me. Never could." He grips my hand. "Like I said, you tell her."

"From you," I say. "She needs to hear it from you."

"Too late."

"She'll be here soon."

Richard coughs hard then and leans away from me to spit out the rottenness he brings up. He rests against the grave marker and gasps.

"Have you decided?" He asks the question of me again when he can. "About life? What you want to do with yours?"

"I'm thinking on it," I say. "Maybe there's light at the end of the tunnel."

"Good."

We sit quiet for a bit before Richard speaks again. "My father always told me, *Can't go through life like it's all for your pleasure, Richard.* Told me again and again that, in the end, *You've got to count for something, Richard, or else what's the point?*" He stops talking and breathes several recuperative breaths. "Until you came looking for me…" He coughs a gagging cough. "Until then, I knew my father would turn away from me sad and disappointed if he was here." After each sentence, he pauses and breathes in slowly until his lungs have taken in all the air there is room for.

"So when you hunted me down to say I meant something good in your life…it was," he grunted a laugh, "was something I could put in my baby book. Like I did count for something good, huh? Hear that, Dad?"

"Richard," I say, "there was never a question of that. I mean, god, I'm here because you stood for something to me a lifetime ago. And still do. To me, to everyone."

He hums. "To Andrea?"

"Once she knows the truth she will…she'll be released, knowing her mother was spared further agony."

"You'll tell her," he says.

I hear the siren, its urgent warble a muted alarm in the distance.

"No, you…she'll be here," I insist.

He rolls his head toward me. "I'm going, Edmund."

"No. Wait. Listen. Hear that? They're almost here. You'll be okay."

Those thin lips of his turn up in a sweet smile. "I can go now."

I take hold of his arm and open my mouth to protest. He raises a hand. "You have to decide, Edmund. Where you're going from here."

I give him an awkward embrace, sitting there on the ground. "I'll be all right now, Richard."

He inhales. "That's good. That's good."

I force a laugh. "Aren't we a pair? Floundering around needing something, someone to latch on to and all the while it was us—each other."

Richard's good eye closes; he nods and seems to drift off.

"And Andrea," I say. "She needs you too, really. She'll be here soon."

"Yes, I know." He pats me on the back and says, "One more thing. Twyla. She's afraid of most things. Go easy."

"She's crazy."

"That too, but she cared for me. And I guess in some way we cared about each other—crazy or not."

The sound of the siren rises.

———

The ambulance is here. It's ironic, this flurry of life thundering over an orderly field of death. In they come; I am brushed back by the force of it. Two EMTs crouch over Richard and talk to him kindly, in loud voices, try to rouse him. He licks his lips and moves his head in wan acquiescence. They lift him onto a gurney, cover him with a blanket, and bark questions at me: "How did the bruises occur. What are his health problems?" I tell them that he has lung disease; I don't tell them Twyla bashed in his face. The EMTs, a woman and a man, work in choreographed syncopation; they wrench Richard's shirt open, buttons popping off, and attach wired patches to his chest and stare at the screen on the portable heart monitor. Richard's one good eye flutters open, he sees me, his lips arch up slightly, then he is gone. I know he's gone; it just isn't over electronically. The woman EMT raises her voice, "We're losing him, we're losing him." I watch them insert IVs into each lifeless arm; then I turn away, my head swimming. Behind me the language is clipped, economical: the man is doing CPR; the woman is watching the line fluttering on the monitor and checking the IVs.

They finally concede to what I've known and stand down; the victim is dead, *coded,* as they say. Andrea is there when I turn away, standing next to the guy with the Suburban, staring past the granite headstone at the lifeless form of a man she used to know and love. Richard Avery Vickerman is dead. I lurch across two graves moaning her name; her legs give way before I get to her. The guy reaches out and keeps her from falling. When I get to her, she fights me.

"No, no, no." She slaps me on the chest with an open hand again and again. "Damn him, not now." She puts a hand to her mouth and closes her eyes and leans against me. We stand that way, and the emergency people stand almost at military rest and wait. After several minutes, the male EMT comes over and whispers that they have to wait until the police send out an officer designated as a medical examiner to declare the deceased— deceased. So we wait more. For a bit we are distracted by the procedural packing up of the ambulance gear and then by Andrea's sudden outburst that she has to see her father before he is carted away.

She pulls away from me and approaches the blanketed gurney on heeled shoes that sink in the soft sod. The female EMT lifts the blanket and pulls it back. Andrea looks down for a long moment, sags against the cart, then collects herself and comes back to where I'm standing, her face void of expression. The huddle of people is one of those awkward assemblages that occur at times like this, people who don't fit together; but there they are, anyway, part of someone else's unbearable pain.

A patrol car arrives after about twenty minutes of waiting and murmuring and pacing. Andrea and I and the Suburban guy watch as the policeman confers with the ambulance crew and checks whatever it is you check.

"It's not him," Andrea says while we observe the steps being taken to declare her father dead. "After all this time, it's not even him."

"Sure it is," I say. "What do you mean?"

"No," she says. "I looked, but I can't see my father."

"It's the bruises. And because he was so awful sick. But he's Dick Vic all right."

She smiles at that. "Haven't heard Dick Vic for a long time. He didn't even want to see me. Did he? Did he hate me? Is that why he ran off, ran away from the thought of seeing me?"

I say no, he didn't hate her, and consider how I am going to tell her the whole of it. Then it's all over. Richard is zipped into a body bag, loaded, and the ambulance drives away. Its tires making depressions in the grass. The guy with the Suburban takes us back up to Mississippi Avenue. We lock up the house with our promise to one another to return and pack up Richard's effects— thunder eggs and all—later, not now. Driving through Vernonia this time, I feel like I did as a kid when my folks moved the family someplace else—I don't belong there anymore. Andrea puts her hand on my thigh as we drive away; I grab and don't let go.

————————

In Manning the parking lot at the nursery is alive with official automobiles: state police and sheriff patrol cars sit side by side. An ambulance, its blue and red lights flashing and rear doors open, is parked by the open gate to the nursery yard. A small cluster of onlookers stands in silence—just watching. I park the Chevelle behind a patrol car, kill the ignition, and jump out. Andrea is right behind me asking me what is wrong several times; she stops when I grip her arm. I'm anxiously looking for someone to talk to, to get the story of just what has happened. Jerry the mechanic is standing on the fringe of the onlookers; he raises a hand. I approach a sheriff's deputy and start asking questions; it turns out he is actually glad to see me. I'm the only person so far who seems connected to the place and seems to know anything. Lucky me.

A customer found Glen lying out in the yard about an hour ago; she has evidently been outside overnight—*just like Richard*, I think. The deputy says she's been beaten, not sure with what yet, adding that she is alive and will be okay according to the ambulance EMTs I tell the deputy and a state patrolman that I'm pretty sure who did it. The deputy jots down the details about Twyla Ann somebody. Never did get her last name—isn't that something? The deputy says that my story jives with what Glen has evidently already told them, but he's glad to have some corroboration. Within minutes an all-points bulletin is out for Twyla. The hunt is on.

Glen is still in the nursery yard on a gurney. I ask the EMT in charge if we can talk to her before they take her away; he gives me a nod. Glen sees Andrea and me approach and manages a smile. Her face is bruised; there is a knot on her forehead and a bandage on one cheek. That's all I can see, other than the IV drip and the line taped to her arm.

She licks her lips and says, "Not drunk."

Man, it feels good to laugh. Andrea laughs, too, just out of relief I think.

Glen looks at me. "It was Twyla. Guess you told her what I said, huh?"

"That bitch. I'm sorry. I didn't figure on this."

"Yeah, well, she wasn't so tough. I got in a lick or two myself. But she had a real shit fit, Twyla. Yelling that I ruined everything, killed off her security and a bunch of stuff I couldn't make out." She grunts a laugh. "We made kindling out of a couple of hoe handles. Guess you can tell who won."

"She has the law on her tail now," I say. "Won't get far."

Glen laughs. "I feel sorry for the badge that catches her. She won't go easy. Say, who is this, anyway?" Glen is squinting up at Andrea.

"This is Andrea, Richard Vickerman's daughter." Glen looks at me then back at Andrea then back at me, and I feel my face flushing. A smile blossoms on Glen's face.

"Andrea," she says, "you're keeping questionable company."

"Actually, I'm his parole officer," Andrea says deadpan.

Glen laughs then starts to cough. "I like her. Did you find your dad?"

Andrea swallows. "He…he's gone," she says. "He died."

"Oh geez," Glen croaks. She looks at me. "Twyla do it?"

"Yeah, she worked him over, too. But he was real sick, and it was too much."

Glen coughs again, and the EMT signals that they have to go.

"I'll take care of things here," I say as they start to take her away.

"Try not to run me into bankruptcy 'fore I get back, will ya?"

Andrea and I watch Glen being loaded into the ambulance. I

get in one last wave to her before the doors close and the siren starts. Then she is gone; the fading wail of the siren is the only evidence of her battle with Twyla. The police put up Crime Scene yellow tape, cutting off any access to the yard; that would have upset Glen no end—might lose a sale to all those potential customers hanging around. But people can only stand around out of curiosity so long until one by one they drift off. The locals are walking back to their homes and businesses, and others are starting cars and driving away—show's over.

Andrea and I go into the shop and wait in silence, unable or unwilling to talk about the last two days. I'm rearranging merchandise on the shelves for the third time when the deputy sheriff I'd talked with earlier comes in and says they're done. I thank him and close gate to the yard, padlock it, and lock the shop.

I'll be back tomorrow.

Epilogue

It took a couple of months, but the authorities brought Twyla to ground just outside Pocatello, Idaho. She was working as a live-in housekeeper for a retired widower rancher. She'd already taken over his finances and was limiting folks from visiting the old guy. Bitch—a real piece of work. But an old drinking buddy of the ranch owner got suspicious and tipped the law. Twyla didn't go peaceful. No sir. Took three of Bannock County's finest to subdue the woman, with her inflicting at least one black eye, a groin injury and scratches to faces that later became infected, so the story goes. A picture appeared in The Oregonian of an enraged Twyla A. Crocker in restraints, glaring into the camera as she was being wrestled into the courthouse. Her mouth wide open, her big nose wrinkled in a snarl—the only thing missing was fangs. Twyla Ann, sorry I knew you.

Glen was in St. Vincent Hospital only three days but stayed in bed in her trailer for another four. Meanwhile, yours truly showed up every day and kept the nursery going pretty well, if I do say so. In fact, business was quite brisk while Glen was out of order because people had read of the assault in the paper or heard about it on the local TV news—fitting nicely into the media's if-it-bleeds-it-leads formula. Then, again, when Glen was able to start hobbling about the yard, people came by to see her first hand—using a cane was her idea, great touch. Later, when Twyla was captured in Idaho, we had another burst of business. Glen is suggesting that I volunteer to be robbed and beaten sometime soon.

So, yeah, I'm working full time for Glen these days. We're learning some marketing tricks from Andrea, a master at selling sizzle; in fact she's sending us customers from among her home buyers and sellers. After all, whether selling or buying a house, nothing spruces up its appearance or sales potential like some eye-catching flowers and shrubs. We're getting the hang of it. I'm even thinking of approaching Amalgamated-Durant about wholesaling plants to their customers. Wouldn't that be sweet?

I'm no longer living in the old apartment. Andrea finally visited the place after Richard died. She grimaced; she actually grimaced. Then she smiled sweetly, kissed me, and told me I mustn't live there anymore. I moved out and into the Tudor. We've decided to take a chance on each other and see how it goes; I think we both have good vibes about it. I'm learning what I don't know about running a nursery. Andrea's still selling real estate—our cash cow—but she works with me and gets dirt under her nails more and more.

I still smile about the moment I went to see Felix and told him that I was giving up my apartment. We were sitting out on his balcony drinking the beer I'd brought and had just watched Lolita stroll by on lubricated hinges when he hummed his appreciation, burped, and said, "Well, you found your guy, and now look at you, right back in the thick of it. That what you want?"

"Yeah," I said, "sleeping nights, getting up before noon, got things I want to do and a partner in all that. Someone I care about, as a matter of fact. You ought to try it."

"Ah gawd," he groaned, "yer making my teeth come loose."

"What about that retired schoolteacher?" I asked.

"Sorry about your guy dying on ya," he said, ignoring my question. "Worked, though, for him and you, huh?"

"It did," I answered. "It really did."

Felix took another pull on the bottle, set it down beside his chair, and folded his hands in his lap. "Wished it coulda been like that for me and old Stoddard. Damn him, anyway."

"When's he getting out?" I asked.

"Hell, been out for eight months or more."

We sat looking out over the yard. Crows were making a racket—I didn't care. "Felix," I said finally, "go look him up."

"Nah, can't do that," he said with no oomph to it.

"Why not?" I asked.

"Schoolteacher?" he said, fending off another of my questions. "She still smiles at me." He laughed. "Dang, she must be desperate."

"Felix, I have a question for you," I said right then.

He moaned. "Not another one."

"This is about the car, the Chevelle," I said. "I want to buy it from you."

"You can't afford it," he answered flat out. "Checked on that. Dang, those old muscle cars are worth big bucks now. Can't just give 'er away."

"I want it. Will you sell it to me or not? What do you want for it?"

He told me what he could likely get for it; I sucked a lot of air on that figure. Then he told me what he'd sell it to me for—still out of my league. Finally, he asked what I had on me in cash. I opened my wallet and pulled out eighteen dollars. "Down payment," he said.

After we finished off the beers, he handed me the title to the car, and we shook hands on the deal. Come to find out he'd been carrying insurance on the car the whole time I thought I was running bare. He followed me out to the parking lot and patted the Chevelle on the hood.

"I may see if I can find old Stoddard," he said and walked away.

I hollered after him, but he just kept going at his usual pace.

There is something special about what I'm doing now: growing things and helping others grow things, too. Glen, she has been trying to teach me the ways of becoming a nurseryman—in her no-nonsense manner. We're coming along. When school was out, I asked Glen if my son could come work for us that summer instead of flipping burgers or whatever he was doing. She grunted but agreed, and darned if he didn't say yes when I asked him. He stayed with Andrea and me; that was interesting but actually worked out fine. Ended up being the closest I've ever been with Tommy. Samantha and her husband stopped by once on their way to the beach, looked around, and wrinkled up their noses. One for two isn't bad. I think Samantha really just wanted to crow that her mother had gotten married to an attorney from Tacoma and that he had taken her to Paris for their honeymoon. Go, Sylvia!

Unbelievably, one day Felix actually left the compound and paid for a cab ride all the way out to Manning. Just had to see what had come of me. Told the cab to wait while he poked around and had a beer with Glen and me in her trailer, which he found almost as comfortable as his apartment. When he was leaving, I followed him out; and, before he got into the waiting cab, he told me that he had looked up his old shop teacher, Stoddard, after all.

"Wasn't no dang celebration," he said, "but, who knows, maybe we can do it again."

Andrea and I are getting used to cooperative housekeeping again. It's pretty easy, actually, when the other person really wants to be with you. Hell, I don't know what all of this means.

Guess I should send a dozen roses to Sylvia for kicking me loose and a case of Oregon wine to that attorney she married. But mostly I feel certain that Richard's father had it as close as it gets. It may not be earth shaking, my life, but it could be that I'm counting for something.

Eventually I called my father. I put it off as long as I could, but I had to do it. He listened quietly while I told him what had happened to Dick Vic.

"That's fine, Edmund," he said. "He was a good man. Are you okay now?"

I assured him that I was. It's strange for a father and son to discover each other so late in life, but we've begun. He is even talking about he and mom coming to Portland and taking a look at the nursery.

Of course, every once in awhile, I do recall those lethargic mornings just lying in bed watching Martha make magic with carpet scraps.

# # #

GEORGE BYRON WRIGHT is the author of the Oregon Trio, a unique body of work comprised of three novels set in the small towns of his youth. *Baker City 1948* was published first, followed by *Tillamook 1952,* and *Roseburg 1959. Driving to Vernonia* is his fourth novel. He lives with his wife and first reader, Betsy, in Portland, Oregon.